WELCOME

ACCIDENTAL MYSTERY SERIES

THE WRATH OF GRAPES

EVELYN ALLEN HARPER

To: Ellie —
Keep reading!
Evelyn Allen Harper

ISBN 978-1-61434-285-4

Printed in the United States of America.

BookLocker.com, Inc.
2011

First Edition

ACKNOWLEDGEMENTS

THE TITLE, THE PLOT, and the first chapter of the third book of The Accidental Mystery Series came to me one morning between waking and sleeping. Knowing that dreams have a way of evaporating if you don't grab them immediately, I ran past my husband on my way to the computer yelling, "Don't talk to me!"

The setting for the first two books, And So To Sleep and And So To Dream, was a small western Michigan town. The first chapter of The Wrath of Grapes that I was typing that morning took the story to a vineyard on the peninsula. The realization that now I had to do research on vineyards and the growing of wine grapes wasn't making me happy.

I have sung with the Sweet Adeline International organization for years. That night at rehearsal, a guest stood up and introduced herself.

"Hello," she said. "My name is Sharon Laing, and my husband and I own a vineyard."

Talk about serendipity! So thank you, Sharon, for being my source of information about life and work on the vineyard.

I appreciate all of you who have read my manuscript and made suggestions. In my writing group, I am fortunate that there is one who hates prepositional phrases, one who frowns on adverbial phrases, and one who strikes out conjunctions. I'm lucky to have a friend who attacks all unnecessary commas.

Special thanks go to those who edited my manuscript with lots of red marks and cross-outs: Jean Bryant, Sue Jones, Jody Clark, Diane Clark, Pat Bell, Karen Fritz, and Barry Harper, my husband.

ABOUT THE AUTHOR

EVELYN LIVES WITH HER husband, Barry, in a home they built on the shores of lovely Pearl Lake near Empire, Michigan. She loves pets and currently shares her home with Earl, a dog from the Humane Society, and Simon, a cat that coyotes were eyeing for lunch.

The daughter of a coal miner, Evelyn left the hills of Pennsylvania to attend Anderson College in Indiana and then to Michigan where she earned a Masters at Wayne State University.

She taught school until the birth of her two children, Jill and Tom. A constant delight in her life is her stepdaughter, Judith.

A Realtor for many years, some of Molly's real estate adventures happened to Evelyn, but most are fiction.

When a condition called Restless Legs interferes with her sleep, Evelyn finds that writing helps get her through the night. The Wrath of Grapes is the third book in The Accidental Mystery Series.

CONTACT THE AUTHOR

EVELYN WOULD LOVE TO hear from you.

If you have comments on The Wrath of Grapes, the third book in The Accidental Mystery Series, contact her at evharp@hotmail.com

Find out more about her on her website: www.evelynallenharper.com

THE WRATH OF GRAPES

CHAPTER 1

LOOKING BACK, Sarah didn't know why she wasn't more suspicious of Frank's behavior when he returned from town on Saturday. He had been pleasant enough during the weeks she had catered to him while he was recovering from his injuries, but as soon as he started to feel better, his attitude changed. Some days he was downright nasty. It got so bad on that Saturday when he yelled that she was suffocating him, she was glad to see him head for town. Watching him leave, she wondered why she had ever thought he was good looking. In the short time he had been with her, he had even developed a pot gut.

It had taken some time to get over the fascination of watching him constantly rubbing his tongue over his broken front teeth, but when she did, she became fixated on his strange head of hair: the crown was gray, the ends were blonde. Sarah was so lonely and, needing help with the vines, she had overlooked all his faults. Since trying to run the vineyard alone was overwhelming, she prayed that if she made it pleasant enough Frank would stick around.

ONE SNOWY NIGHT in early November as she was driving past the scenic lookout on Route 116, she thought the rather large lump in the middle of the road was a deer from the herd that hung around that area.

Intending to steer around it, she changed her mind when she saw a shoeless foot sticking out of the ball of snow.

The shoeless foot turned out to be attached to a half-frozen and injured man who claimed, when she managed to rouse him, that he was the victim of a hit-and-run accident. Knowing that the combination of a dark night, a lone woman, and a strange man held the ingredients for possible gory headlines in the morning paper, Sarah had a decision to make. Since she didn't have a cell phone and there were no houses nearby, she had struggled over her options: she could leave him and hope the next car would stop, or she could be a Good Samaritan. Throwing caution and her better judgment aside, she had chosen to be a Good Samaritan.

Insisting that all he needed was a bit of first aid, the man had refused to let her take him to the hospital. Instead, he asked that she take him home with her. Sarah knew that she hadn't resisted the notion very hard. Aside from his apparent injuries, he was a fine specimen of a man, a potential worker for her vineyard.

Last harvest season when they were up to their necks in ripe grapes, her husband Larry had the audacity to up and die on her for no good reason. Now, every morning when Sarah woke up alone and faced the unending job of tending to the vineyard without his help, she got angry with Larry all over again

That Saturday, when he didn't think she was looking, she had watched Frank put a small leather pouch into his pocket. She knew what was in that pouch because she had given it to him; it contained a razor, soap, a toothbrush, toothpaste, and a comb. When he left, she had the suspicion that Frank would not be returning to her.

HE DID RETURN. Something had happened in town that had given him a huge attitude adjustment. The Frank who had walked back into her kitchen late that afternoon was as jolly as old St. Nick himself. When she asked him if he was practicing being Santa, his big laugh and hearty "Ho, ho, ho" response was so over the top that she moved closer to him in an attempt to smell his breath.

While Sarah fixed soup and sandwiches, he hung around the kitchen telling her about the second Christmas parade. She was confused because she hadn't been aware that there had been a first Christmas parade. Sarah had dropped the newspaper subscription and hadn't replaced the television set after its and Larry's untimely demises. The vineyard was so far out on the peninsula that she didn't make the trip into town often enough to know what was going on. He didn't know too much about what had happened either, but he had picked up the information by listening to conversations around him. It seemed a huge dog had mauled the first Santa and wrecked that parade.

Frank waited until they were at the table before he started to outline the work that had to be done on the vines this time of year and how they should go about doing it. Sarah almost dropped her spoon into her soup. With no newspaper to read or television to watch, she *had* seen him reading books from Larry's library. Up until now when she tried to get him to help her, he'd look at her with disdain and walk away.

Acting as if this had been his job all along, he picked up the drying cloth and helped Sarah with the dishes. However, it was the friendly pat on her shoulder at bedtime as they went their separate ways that really puzzled her.

Something *big* must have happened in town.

CHAPTER 2

IN THE MORNING before the alarm went off, Sarah was dreaming of having breakfast with Larry, her dearly departed husband. In the dream she was smiling at his handsome face as he poured freshly brewed coffee into her cup. The smell of coffee and the sound of sizzling bacon were so real, she pulled the covers over her head and settled back to enjoy the dream a bit longer. It was the clatter of dishes that jarred her awake. Sitting up in bed, she no longer was interested in her dream. *Nobody cooks in this house but me, so what is going on in my kitchen?*

Not bothering with how she looked, she threw on some clothes, rushed down the stairs, and charged into the kitchen. There was Frank, wearing her apron while holding a spatula in one hand and a skillet full of eggs and bacon in the other. Flashing his jagged-toothed grin at her, he wished her good morning and invited her to breakfast. Sarah was speechless. Still having trouble connecting the Frank she was looking at now with the Frank of yesterday, she hesitated but a moment. She might be suspicious of what Frank was up to, but that was no reason to turn down a perfectly good breakfast.

Joining her at the table, Frank made small talk while they ate, which was something he had never done before. He cleared the table while Sarah had a second cup of coffee. Again, they ended up doing the dishes together. The conversation they had while he washed and Sarah dried was about the vineyard. All of a sudden, well, at least since late yesterday afternoon, Frank's interest in grapes was all-consuming. He obviously had learned from Larry's books.

Because Larry had been the grape person, it was his fault that Sarah, who had no great love of grapes, found herself the sole owner of a successful vineyard. His Uncle Paul had started the vines many years ago. Paul and Larry's father were brothers. It took only one summer vacation working at the vineyard to instill in Larry the love of growing grapes. After that, he spent every summer working with his uncle.

LARRY AND SARAH HAD met by the water cooler one day at work. She was the new paralegal secretary at a large Birmingham law firm, and Larry was just one of many young attorneys vying for a chance to be made partner. She clearly remembered that meeting. Stepping back from the cooler with a cup of water in his hand, Larry had cocked his head and slowly swept his eyes over her as she walked by. She could have been offended, but she wasn't. Sarah had held her head high as he took in her slim body, her perfectly coifed hair, her manicured nails, and her expertly made-up face. She was flattered by the attention of such a handsome young lawyer, and Larry certainly *was* handsome. Becoming an exclusive couple almost immediately, a lovely wedding wasn't far behind.

With a big send-off after the reception, did they go on a honeymoon to some romantic place? Did they go on a lovely cruise to the tropics? No, they went, and she was still angry about this, to Uncle Paul's vineyard. Their honeymoon was spent walking through the vines with Uncle Paul while he explained his expansion ideas to Larry. The vineyard was thriving and finally making money. He had a contract with a local winemaker to take everything he harvested. The last couple of years the weather had cooperated; the crops had been heavy.

It was a good thing that Uncle Paul had shared his expansion ideas with Larry, because Paul died suddenly a few months after their visit. Now that she thought about it, maybe dying suddenly was a family trait. Since Uncle Paul had no children, they ended up being owners of the vineyard.

THE EARLY MONTHS of the year are pruning time for the vines. Today, however, because they were recovering from a record snowfall and the temperature was frigid, Frank and Sarah didn't brave the cold. They spent the afternoon working on a thousand-piece puzzle on a card table in front of a blazing fireplace. The evening found them laughing around the same card table while drinking margaritas and playing a cutthroat game of gin. Frank hung onto her every word, laughing at her jokes. She actually caught him cheating at cards. He wasn't cheating to win; he was cheating to make it easier for her to win. Sarah kept her mouth shut and just watched while they played until they were both tired of the game. She gathered up the cards while he cleared off the card table and took the margarita glasses to the kitchen.

Tonight, when they parted for their separate bedrooms, the previous pat on the shoulder turned into a full body hug.

CHAPTER 3

SARAH WASN'T SURPRISED when she again woke to the smell of brewing coffee. Reaching out, she turned off the alarm clock before it had a chance to ring. She hadn't always hated that sound. Larry used to set the alarm to ring fifteen minutes before they absolutely had to get out of bed. Remembering what they did in those fifteen minutes still left her breathless. Her only defense against that overwhelming grief was to be enraged at him for dying on her. She'd fed on that anger; it was the fuel that got her through the day.

Today, before going downstairs to see what Frank was cooking, she spent a little time on her appearance. The mirror-reflected image wasn't kind. Sarah's wide hazel-green eyes, once prized as her best feature, were circled with dark rings. Those eyes swept over her reflection, looking for the body that had attracted Larry. It wasn't there. Hard work had taken away the padding on her tall frame; she had more angles than curves. Her black hair was beyond redemption, but using the brush, she tried to tame the tangled curls. Then she surprised herself by picking up a tube of lip-gloss, something she hadn't bothered with for months. This turn of events puzzled her. Although Frank had been living with her for some time, she had never given a thought to her appearance before.

When she walked into the kitchen, she saw a stack of pancakes and a plate of sunny-side-up eggs on the table. Sarah sucked in a quick breath when she noticed that the table had a centerpiece; a vase with one red rose. When had he gone into town for the rose? Frank stood in the middle of the kitchen, proudly wearing her apron that cleverly covered his baby-potbelly.

Over breakfast, they engaged in small talk before the subject of the vineyard came up. Uncle Paul originally had 2,000 plants, but the expansion he had talked to Larry about on their honeymoon had more than doubled that number. Working from dawn to dusk, Larry and Sarah had barely kept up with the demands of the vines.

Frank had obviously been doing his homework. Over the last cup of coffee, he talked to her about setting up a pruning schedule. He spoke, sounding as if he were reading the information out of a book, about how new vines needed to be pruned differently than older vines. He asked her if there was a layout of the vineyard showing the year the vines had been planted. Sarah didn't know if there was such a thing. Her head was spinning from all the information that was spilling out of his mouth. Frank had managed to learn a lot about the vines in such a short time. Sarah was both amazed and puzzled.

Since today was a much milder day than yesterday, they bundled up and headed to the vines with their pruning instruments. He worked rings around her. When they broke for a late lunch, she was amazed at how much they had accomplished. There was some money in her budget to hire harvest-help in the fall, but there was no money available to hire help for pruning. Now, Sarah looked at Frank with different eyes. Since Larry's death, the overwhelming task of maintaining the vineyard had turned her nightly prayers into a plea to God, beseeching him to send her help. Was Frank God's answer to her prayers?

Around four o'clock they quit and headed for the house.

They were so tired that, after putting away the supper dishes, they bumped into each other on the way to their separate bedrooms. Giggling like school kids when they parted, the previous pat on the shoulder of one night that had turned into a full body hug the next night, became a quick peck on Sarah's cheek tonight.

CHAPTER 4

SAMMY THE GRUNT, for that's who Frank really was, chuckled every time he thought about the effect that one red rose had had on Sarah. Buying her anything was the last thing on his mind, and that was not why he had sneaked into town. He'd been known to come up with brilliant ideas, and that was one of them. God, that bitch was easy to impress!

He had found out that Saturday, after making the grand exit from Smothering Sarah, that two of his old gang members were looking for him. Before the feds caught them, the three of them had buried a box of drug money and stolen identities in McGuire's cherry orchard. Although they all had sworn that when they got out they would divide the contents of the box equally, Sammy never had any intention of sharing. Not only was he spending the money freely, he had deposited most of it in a bank account that he opened using one of the stolen identities. His plan, after leaving the vineyard, was to empty the bank account, take what was left in the box, and disappear.

What he found was a box empty of everything except a message addressed to him, Sammy the Grunt. His two former gang members were now out of prison. Needing money and identities, they had headed straight for the box. The note clearly stated what the two planned on doing to him when they found him, and they assured him that they *would* find him. He didn't doubt that for a moment. That's when he had fled back to Clutching Sarah. Sammy had shuddered to think about returning to her, but once again, a brilliant idea had popped out of nowhere. Becoming the *sole* owner of a successful vineyard was the new plan.

He knew Sarah was surprised to see him when he walked back into her kitchen, to say nothing about how puzzled she must be about his sudden change of attitude.

He was on his way into town again to see if he could spot his two former friends. The last time they had seen him in prison he had looked like a god. They wouldn't recognize him now. To help matters he hadn't shaved or washed his hair in several days. Fortunately, today was a sunny day and he could wear sunglasses to hide his eyes. Since Larry's coat was too small for him, he made sure it hung open to show the pants that exaggerated his new potbelly. He also intended to smile every chance he got. They wouldn't know him, but he sure as hell would know them.

WHILE WALKING PAST the office of Allen Real Estate, he looked inside and saw Miss Piggy sitting at her desk. Only she didn't look like Miss Piggy any more. Who would have thought there was a good-looking broad under all that padding? For the life of him, he couldn't remember her real name, but he did remember making up a story about his dear dead mother having the same name. Thinking of his mother made him sad. The last time he heard from her she had just gotten out of solitary, her punishment for starting a riot over burned rice pudding. Mom never took to jail time very well.

Not finding Clarence and Albert, he headed back to his truck. He was sure Sarah had already started pruning and was probably pissed that he wasn't there to help. That was when he looked up and saw the redheaded snitch in his police officer's uniform walking toward him. Ducking into the doorway of a little shop, Sammy watched as the snitch waved to someone across the street.

The sweet smell of chocolate hit his nose as he entered the store. Another brilliant idea flew into his head.

If Sarah had been pleased with one red rose, a chunk of Mackinaw Fudge should make her ecstatic.

CHAPTER 5

"HI, TOM!"

The tall redheaded cop winced as he turned his head to see his mother, Peggy, stepping out of the Allen Real Estate office. Struggling to hide a painful grimace, he smiled and waved.

Tom had spent time recovering from an almost fatal stab wound after Sammy the Grunt attacked him at an open house. Since this was his first day back at work, he wasn't about to give his mom a reason to question his recovery. With a big grin on his face, he stopped walking and waited for her to catch up. Hugging her, Tom marveled at the change in his mom since she had taken the receptionist job at Allen Real Estate. Today, she actually looked bubbly. He hadn't seen her this animated since before his dad's death five years ago.

Offering his arm, he exclaimed, "Lucky lady! Since today is the annual Police Department's Take your Mother to Lunch Day, may I please have that honor?"

Peggy, her unruly cloud of dark curls bouncing, laughed and lightly punched his shoulder. "I'd love to, but won't people think I'm in police custody?"

"Don't worry. I'll remember to take off your handcuffs when the food arrives," teased Tom as he opened the door and the two walked into the crowded diner.

While scanning the room, trying to find an empty table, Tom's eyes landed on two men who looked vaguely familiar. As one of the few police officers in this small northern Michigan town, he knew almost everyone. These two men stuck out like thumbs with band-aids on them. Their ill-fitting clothes, their pallor, and the way their shoulders hunched protectively over their food, shouted *prison* to him. Who were they and what were they doing in town? He knew he was right when they spotted his uniform and dropped their eyes.

Peggy, seeing familiar faces, grabbed her son's hand. Puzzling over why the two men looked familiar, Tom wasn't paying attention to where his mom was dragging him until he bumped into a baby stroller.

"Way to go, Bro!" laughed Tom's redheaded sister, Molly. Regaining his balance, Tom looked up and saw her and her detective husband, Mitch. Of course, the stroller held the twins. "And I promise you, if you woke them up, you're in big trouble!"

Looking dapper in his tailored suit, the tall, blue-eyed and handsome Mitch stood, shook Tom's hand, and kissed Peggy on the cheek. "Pull up chairs and sit down. Have lunch with us?"

"What a nice surprise! Until I met Tom, I thought I was going to eat alone. He claims this is the annual Police Department's Take your Mother to Lunch Day." Peggy laughed, as she sat down on the chair that Tom held for her.

There was a time a short while ago when Mitch wasn't Tom's favorite person. All her life Molly had trouble sleeping. She had no idea why her legs made her leap out of bed to walk until she'd sold a house to a sleep doctor. At the sleep clinic open house, she had picked up a pamphlet entitled, "You Are Not Alone". Opening it up, she'd read, "It's bedtime and you want to go to sleep, but your legs won't let you." Never knowing that other people had legs like hers, Molly was astounded when she read that one out of every ten people has some degree of the problem. The condition is called Restless Legs Syndrome, or, after the doctor who first gave it a name, the Ekbom Disease. There's no cure, but a medication containing a dopamine agonist, a drug that mimics bodily chemicals, makes sleep possible. For the first part of her marriage to Mitch, life was wonderful until she became pregnant and couldn't take the prescription. Mitch thought love alone would make her stay in bed beside him. Because that wasn't possible, the marriage almost broke up before the twins were born. Tom still had a hard time completely forgiving Mitch.

"Things still busy at my office?" Molly asked her mother.

"I think you're going to have to hire another salesperson. Clara is about at the end of her rope. If Marilyn and I hadn't stepped in when we did, I don't know what would have happened."

"But there's a problem with just hiring anyone," Molly pointed out. "Clara and the dog are the reason for all the business. It's bad enough that Lucky is spending most of his time with Joe at the fire station."

"Speaking of Joe, anything happening there?" Mitch asked.

"He sure hangs around a lot!" Peggy grinned. "Bringing Lucky in for a visit is always a good excuse. He also is kept pretty busy putting up signs on people's property when Clara lists a house."

"Have you seen Clara recently?" Molly questioned. "I hardly recognized her last time I saw her. She seems to be melting away!"

It hadn't been that long ago since Tom, while in the police academy, had been assigned to be Mitch Hatch's plant in a local gang of boys who were terrorizing Molly's neighborhood. However, shortly after he had joined, three thugs appeared in town with the intent of expanding their drug trade; they used the local boys as their runners. A double murder in McGuire's Alley had placed Molly in danger when she was seen walking in the area that night.

Today Tom was sharing the lunch table with the result of that walk, because that's how detective Mitch and his sister Molly had found each other.

"Earth to Tom! Come back any time now!" Tom shook his head and smiled at Molly. She could always tell when his thoughts were far away.

"Mitch," Tom asked, "did you get a good look at those two men at the window table?"

"Can't say that I did. Why?"

"Just a feeling. Probably nothing important, but I think I've seen them before. So what's the special today?"

"Where's our waitress?" Molly whined. "I'd like to order and get to eat in peace before the twins wake up."

"And I have to get back to work. Oh, here she comes," exclaimed Peggy.

"You still haven't told me what the special is today," Tom complained.

"Try the peanut butter and jelly sandwich," his mom joked. Those sandwiches were about all she had made in her kitchen since her husband died. It was now a family joke.

As the waitress arrived to take the orders, Tom saw the chubby guy from the window table look over his shoulder in his direction as they left the diner.

CHAPTER 6

"WAIT UP FOR ME, ALBERT!" panted Clarence as he ran out the diner's door on the heels of his buddy.

"Step on it, Clarence! I think I seen the waitress lookin' this way!"

"I'm more worried about that cop. Did he look familiar to you?"

"I didn't want him to catch me lookin' at him. Who did he look like?" Albert panted.

"If I knew, I wouldn't have asked you," puffed Clarence. Little rivulets of sweat were running down his chubby cheeks.

"We had enough money to pay for lunch, but that cop spooked me," Albert admitted. "I don't know how many restaurants they have in this hick town, but we can't keep runnin' out without payin' the bill."

Clarence was bent over, still trying to catch his breath. "Sammy sure pulled a fast one on us. That bastard! I'm gonna make him sorry he was ever born. Where the hell did he go?"

"Clarence, he stole almost all of the money that was in that box, so I imagine old Sammy could be just about anywhere right now."

"So if he ain't here, why are we hangin' around?"

"Do you ever listen to yourself, Clarence? How many times have you counted the money that was left?"

"Don't yell at me, Albert."

"Sorry. I'm as mad as you are. We've got to find some way of gettin' our hands on enough money to get out of this town."

Clarence thought that Sammy the Grunt was the best, but Albert's stories about his own dark past in another gang made him almost as good. Hanging around with him had some drawbacks, though. Being with Albert on the night of the two murders in McGuire's Alley had been a big mistake. Even though Sammy had done the killing, the three of them had landed in prison.

To save what little money that was left, the men had been sleeping in a barn, washing up in any restroom they could find, and running out of restaurants without paying. For transportation, they had stolen two bicycles that they repainted red. They had found the can of paint, along with a brush, in the barn.

Retrieving their stolen bikes from the rack, they rode side by side through town. "How are we gonna get some money?" Clarence asked, pedaling hard. "Are we gonna have to get a job?"

"We just have to be creative," Albert answered.

A display of shiny red apples caught Albert's eye. A sign propped beside the apples declared: "Enjoy a Free Apple from Weber's Orchard!"

"Hey Clarence!" he yelled as he rode his bike onto the sidewalk. "How would a nice juicy apple taste right now? Watch this!"

Just as he stretched out his hand to snatch the apple, the door of Allen Real Estate opened. A leashed huge dog and a tall man with thinning black hair stepped out. Slamming on the brakes to avoid them, Albert went sailing over the handlebars. Clarence, who had ridden past Albert, looked back over his shoulder and was so shocked at seeing Albert flat on his back that he veered off the sidewalk and smashed into a parked garbage truck.

Albert slowly got to his feet and turned around. The crack of his head on the cement was giving him double vision. The sight of two black bears looking at him made him apprehensive.

"Are you all right?" asked the man who had the bears on a leash. "That was quite a spill."

Albert rubbed his eyes and shook his head. When he looked again, he was relieved to see there was now only one bear staring at him. "I don't think I broke anythin'," he answered nervously. "I'm more concerned about your bear. Is he dangerous?"

The man laughed and held out his hand. "Lucky is a dog, not a bear, and he isn't dangerous. I'm Joe."

The door to Allen Real Estate opened and a pretty woman joined them. "What's all the commotion?" she asked.

"I'm afraid that Lucky and I caused an accident," Joe said. "Clara, why don't you take this one into the office and I'll go check on the other guy." He pointed in the direction of the smashed bicycle and the crumpled figure of a man lying beside it. "I haven't seen him move."

Albert looked where he was pointing and was shocked. Losing a fairly new bicycle like that wasn't good.

Limping for effect, Albert followed Clara into the office. He was sitting in a chair drinking a cup of coffee and eating a homemade brownie when the man who called himself Joe brought a bleeding Clarence through the door. From the look of it, the mishap had done some damage to his friend.

"You hurt bad?" he asked.

"Smashed my nose!" complained Clarence.

"You smashed your bike, too! Way to go, dummy!"

"Ah, don't yell at me," pleaded Clarence as he used his shirtsleeve to wipe the blood off his nose.

"My name is Clara," the pleasant lady said. "I'm the salesperson here at Allen Real Estate. And may I ask your names?"

Alarmed, Clarence and Albert looked at each other. Neither man could remember the name on the stolen ID in his pocket.

Albert did some quick thinking. Previously he had explained to Clarence that, since they might be cornered into difficult situations, they needed to talk about ways to get out of them. Hoping Clarence remembered this one, he nudged him, winked, and doubled over.

"Oh, my!" yelled Clarence, sounding frantic, "he's havin' one of his attacks! I need to get him into the bathroom before he barfs. Please, where is it?"

Clara pointed down the hall and the two men raced to get there. Inside, they collapsed. "That was quick thinkin', Albert!"

"I'm just glad you remembered what to do! Now get out your wallet and see who you are today. I'm George Fritz. Who are you?"

Clarence squinted. "Uh, Albert, the light ain't so good in here. I-I-I can't read it."

Albert had figured out early in their association that Clarence couldn't read. "Give it to me!" he said as he grabbed it out of Clarence's hand. "Looks like you're Ed Crawford from Atlanta, Georgia."

"Damn!" complained Clarence. "Does that mean I have to talk with a southern accent?"

"Do I have to think of everythin'? If they ask, tell them you ain't lived there long enough to get an accent."

"Good thinkin'. Where you from?"

"Detroit, Michigan. Well, since I'm through barfin', let's go and meet our new friends."

CHAPTER 7

CLARA CLARK, THE SALESPERSON at Allen Real Estate, looked up as the two accident victims filed out of the bathroom. The short one who had run into the garbage truck seemed to have recovered faster than the taller one who, according to Joe, had flipped over the handlebars of his bike. She refilled their coffee cups; the plate of brownies was about empty.

As they introduced themselves, it became noticeable that they both looked confused when they were called by name, especially the short chubby one. At one point he had looked around to see who Joe was talking to, and then he got a sheepish grin on his face when he figured out that Joe was talking to him. They both had a stale odor about them that suggested that they hadn't been using any bathing facilities.

Joe tried to get them to talk about themselves, but they seemed more interested in asking about the town. The tall one asked Joe if he had seen any new people. Both men sat up straight when Joe said that he *had* seen someone new just the other day. Clara watched how intently they had waited for Joe to tell them about the new person. When Joe described the guy as a tall, unkempt man with stringy, greasy hair, a pot gut, and missing front teeth, they looked as if someone had just told them that there was no Santa Claus.

When the plate of brownies was empty, George stood up and said, "Ed and me really appreciate you helpin' us, but we gotta go now."

Joe and Clara watched from the window as the two men huddled around Ed's smashed bike. "Looks like they're having a heated conversation about something," Joe commented.

"I hope it's about their next bath! The whole office stinks, and I don't even want to imagine the mess they left in the lavatory. Ugh!"

Joe, who had been looking intently out the window, exclaimed, "Clara, look at the paint job on those bikes."

"What are you now, Joe? An expert on bike painting?" Clara laughed as she poked him in the ribs.

"Yes, and I'm an expert on a few other things. But you'll have to get to know me a bit better to find out what they are." Joe leered as he returned the poke.

Ignoring the innuendo, Clara asked, "So, what is it about the paint job that catches your eye?"

"Okay, here it is. Those bikes are relatively new and shouldn't need to be repainted. But if they did, why would they both be painted with the same exact red color? Think about it."

"I'm thinking." Clara pretended to pucker her brow then, with a sudden flash of certainty on her face, playfully cried, "Because they're not their bikes!"

"Hey, right answer, girl!" Joe laughed as he gave her a high-five. "I don't think there's any doubt; those are stolen bikes. My gut feeling is that those two birds are bad news."

"I think they're in our town looking for someone. Did you watch their faces when you were describing the one strange man in town?"

"If you want to talk about faces, you should have seen how intently George listened to your telephone conversation with Mrs. Cross."

"How so?"

"He could only hear your end of the conversation, but I think his ears twitched when you mentioned that you would watch the Cross house while they were away."

"Really? Usually when I say that I will watch a house for one of my listings, I mean that I will drive by their house at least once a day while they are gone. Think I should do more than that for the Cross house?"

"Probably not. Neither one of those guys looked smart enough to find anything." Joe yawned, then turned and grinned at Clara. "I must say, this little incident was an interesting spot in an otherwise ordinary day."

"What are you up to for the rest of this ordinary day?" questioned Clara.

Joe picked up the signs and headed for the door. "I'll pound these signs in the front yards of your new listings, and then come back for Lucky. I'm on duty tonight."

Clara watched Joe as he walked to his car. Lucky, who had remained quietly in the corner while the two strange men were there, lumbered to her side. Absentmindedly, Clara's hand went down to Lucky's huge head and patted it.

CLARA HAD MET JOE soon after she befriended Lucky, an abused dog that had scratched on her office door. Since the dog wouldn't get into a car, Clara had to walk him back and forth to work. When the walk took them past the fire station, the firemen offered to give Lucky a bath after Clara explained that the owner of Allen Real Estate wasn't going to allow Lucky to stay in the office because he smelled so bad. It turned into quite the scene when, after the dog was wet and soaped-up, he just walked off, dragging several fireman with him. A photographer from the paper happened to drive by, and the picture made it not only on the front-page of the morning paper, but also on the eleven o'clock news on Channel 7. The results of all that free advertising brought so much business Molly had to hire her mother to answer the phones and

Mitch's mother to do computer research. Molly, who was pregnant with twins, was supposed to stay home and off her feet.

Joe was one of the firemen who had helped with the bath, and he and Clara had been friends since that day. When the manager of Clara's condo sent her a notice that Lucky couldn't stay in the condo because he exceeded the size limits, Joe kept him at the fire station. But there was a problem with that. Every time they got a call to go to a fire Jimmy, the fire station's dog, jumped on. Since Lucky refused to get on the truck, he stayed behind and howled until they returned.

Clara smiled when she remembered last year's two Christmas parades. The first one was wrecked because Lucky had jumped onto Santa's fire truck and attacked him. Clara had talked Molly's husband, Detective Mitch Hatch, into getting a search warrant to check out the farm of the man they had hired to play Santa. The conditions at the farm had been so bad that, when it was evident that this was where Lucky had lived before his escape, he got a reprieve from the townspeople. By the time the news and pictures made the paper, Lucky was a hero. That meant more free advertisement for Allen Real Estate and a lot more work for Clara. A second Christmas parade was held because storeowners were upset that they had missed the biggest selling day of the year.

Clara never thought she'd love a dog the way she had come to love Lucky. He stayed at the fire station full time but she saw him when Joe brought him by the office. If Clara wasn't busy, she walked with them. Lately it had been a toss-up as to which one of them she looked forward to seeing most. They both had brought so much change to her life. Lucky was the reason for all the business that had come to Allen Real Estate. Clara was working so hard she kept forgetting to eat, and she found herself losing weight faster than with any diet she had ever been on.

Joe, divorced with two boys, was as jaded as Clara was about any new relationship. It was funny in a way. His two kids were about the same age as Clara's grandkids even though Joe and Clara were the same age. Clara had married young and Joe hadn't.

It was quiet in the office for a change. Clara's thoughts went back to the two men. From the way they were questioning Joe, it had made her think they were looking for someone who might be in town. She didn't know the man Joe had seen the other day, the one he was telling the two guys about. She hadn't seen anyone new in town since Sammy, and no one had seen him since the day he stabbed Tom and broke into this office.

When Lucky heard Joe coming back, he ran to the door. He and Lucky headed for the fire station while Clara drove home to her condo. She had never noticed that she was lonely before but since Lucky had gone to live at the station with Joe, her nights seemed empty.

Empty of what, she wondered.

CHAPTER 8

"WAIT UP!" CLARENCE YELLED at Albert who was pedaling away from him. "It ain't fair!"

Not turning around, Albert yelled back, "What ain't fair, Clarence?"

"You got a bike and I don't."

"Well," puffed Albert, "whose fault is that?"

"Yours!"

"Mine?" Albert screeched to a halt. "How the hell do you figure that?"

"If you hadn't tried that stupid apple snatchin' thing, everythin' would be all right now," puffed Clarence. "I'd still have a bike."

"Clarence, if it was all up to you, we'd be dead of starvation by now."

"How long do you think we're gonna get away with stiffin' the restaurants?" asked Clarence, his chest heaving. "This is a small town, and I'll bet most of the eatin' places are watchin' for us. I sure don't want to go back to jail!"

"Let's go back to the playground and get you another bike and then I'll tell you how we're gonna survive for the next couple of days," Albert said as he easily pulled away from the trotting Clarence.

The bike rack was full, but word must have spread about the two stolen bicycles because all bikes were securely chained and locked.

"Bummer!" Clarence dropped the pieces of his smashed bike.

Laughing, Albert called over from the other side of the rack. "Here's one that ain't locked!" Clarence looked up as Albert rolled a small girl's pink bike toward him.

Stomping his foot, Clarence declared, "I ain't gonna ride that thing!"

"It's either this bike, or you're walkin'!" Albert rang the bike's bell. "Make a choice!"

"Oh, all right." Clarence reluctantly got on the bike and pedaled off, his knees hitting his chin with every rotation. "So when are you gonna tell me about your next big plan?"

Albert wasn't talking because he was laughing.

"Shut up before I punch you in the nose!" Clarence yelled. "So talk."

Albert wiped his eyes. "Did you pay any attention to that lady back there in the office when she was on the phone?"

"No. Did you?"

"That's the difference between me and you," bragged Albert. "I'm always lookin' for angles."

"What kind of angle is she?"

"She's not the angle, stupid! It's what she said. A Mrs. Cross called to say they would be out of town for a couple of days."

"So? We have no idea where this Mrs. Cross lives."

"Come on, Clarence, think! That lady in the office must have the listin' on Mrs. Cross' house."

"So?"

"First, we have to find a phonebook. We look up the name Cross and then write down all the addresses. When we ride past the right house, it will have an Allen Real Estate sign in the front yard."

Clarence stewed a bit over Albert's plan wondering if this one would be as hard on him as the apple-snatching debacle. Nothing bad came to mind, so he chuckled. "I think you have a winner this time!

Now where do we find a phonebook? I sure haven't seen a phone booth in this town. Everyone has cell phones."

"Stores have them, but now we have to come up with a likely story for them to share the phonebook with us. We can't get too specific because everyone knows each other in small towns. If we say like, I'm lookin' for my cousin, Susie Smith, they could say somethin' like, Oh, Susie Smith is my neighbor! Let's call her!"

"So what's the right story?"

"I don't know everythin'!" Albert shrugged. "Let's play it by ear."

Clarence looked aghast at Albert. "You can play your ears?"

"For God's sake, Clarence!"

"Will I like what they play? I'm partial to country."

"I can't believe you've never heard that sayin' before," Albert shook his head. "It just means we do our thing and see where it takes us."

"Just so it's not back to jail." Clarence shuddered.

They parked their bikes outside a hardware store and went inside. Walking up and down the aisles, trying to come up with a good story, they were astonished to see a table stacked high with phonebooks.

Albert came to an abrupt halt. "I don't believe this."

"Don't believe what?" asked Clarence.

"This is almost too easy!" laughed Albert as he picked up a book. "Back up, Clarence."

"Why should I back up?"

"Just do as I say!"

Clarence backed up and Albert stuffed one of the books under the belt on his pants. "So what do we do now?"

"We walk out of here without callin' attention to ourselves." Albert added in a condescending voice, "Think you can do that?"

A cloud crossed Clarence's face. "You don't talk nice to me, Albert. Sometimes you hurt my feelin's."

“Well, then just don’t do anythin’ stupid until we’re out of the store.”

The aisle was long and the book slipped with every step Clarence took. Albert, walking behind him, was appalled to watch the book as it worked its way down to Clarence’s crotch, making him walk funny. The clerk behind the counter was watching the strange pair and wondering if he should offer the short one the use of the store’s private restroom when his phone rang. Albert saw the chance to escape and pushed Clarence toward the door.

“Yes,” they heard the clerk talking on the phone. “The phone company finally dropped off the new books. They’re for the taking, so just come in and pick up as many as you need. They’re taking up too much space, and I need to get rid of them.” He looked over just in time to see what looked like one of those books drop out of the short one’s pant leg. The taller man scooped up the book, slapped the short guy on the back of the head with it, and then both of them ran from the store.

They slowed down outside the store to catch their breath. “Well, wasn’t that special!” a disgusted Albert muttered.

Clarence asked, pointing at Albert’s head. “What just happened in there when you was playin’ your ears?”

“I wasn’t playin’ my ears, Clarence!” Albert said, pushing the offending finger away. “We just stole a free book.”

“Well, that was pretty stupid. Did anyone notice?”

“Why would anyone notice a book fallin’ out of your pant leg?” Albert yelled. “Of course the clerk noticed! How did you let that happen?”

“Let it happen?” Clarence yelled back. “You put it in there, Albert. Why didn’t you put it down your own pants?”

“All right, let’s forget how we got the book. We need to look up all the Cross addresses. If we find the right house and the family has already gone, our troubles will be over for a few days.”

"What do you mean by that?"

"Wouldn't a shower feel good right now? How would you feel about a real bed to sleep in and opening the door of a refrigerator that's full of food?"

Clarence grinned. "You're a genius, Albert! Let's do it!"

CHAPTER 9

SARAH WAS AWAKE BUT SHE still winced when the alarm went off. Sleeping hadn't been easy last night. Tired as she was from working by herself on the vines yesterday, the way Frank had treated her when he returned from town was upsetting enough to keep her awake.

After making a big production of giving her a wedge of fudge, he went to his room. When he came back, it was evident that he had showered and washed his hair. His face was still covered with the beginnings of a beard so maybe he intended to keep it that way. Sometimes working on the vines in cold weather Sarah tied a scarf around her face. Maybe a beard was Frank's version of a scarf. Whatever, that's not what upset her.

The shift in command was changing. Frank was now giving instructions as if he, not Sarah, owned the vineyard.

Maintaining a vineyard is an unending process with no dormant season when you can stop and catch your breath. The vines need constant care. Pruning is very important because an untended vine will grow wild. Frank had picked up the art of pruning much quicker than Sarah had when Larry was teaching her.

So what did Frank do that upset her enough for her to lose sleep? Sarah knew he was reading books on growing wine grapes, so when he came back from town with a catalog that had a big red rose on the cover, she was curious enough to ask him why he had this sudden interest in roses. He informed her that, since it was evident that she didn't know anything, he was taking over and doing whatever was necessary to make the vineyard a success. She was still reeling over that little piece of information when he pulled a paper from his pocket and handed it to her. It was a bill showing he had purchased rosebushes. Rosebushes? He flashed his jagged toothy grin at her, looking as if he were waiting for a pat on the head. Sarah gasped when she saw the bottom figure on the statement because she didn't have money to spend on things not related to the vineyard. That's when he pointed to the spot on the paper that had the word PAID stamped on it. From the look on her face, Frank knew she was puzzled.

Sarah was aware that there are all kinds of pests and diseases that can kill grapevines, but Larry had taken care of that end of the business. Frank took great pride in explaining that the bushes that he would plant in the spring would be like the 'canary in a coal mine'. Because pests love the sweet smell of the roses, they would attack them first. All they had to do was watch what was happening to the roses to get a head start on protecting their grapes. He had bought, with his own money, enough bushes to plant one at the end of each row of vines. Frank was investing in *her* vineyard! She swallowed hard and kept her mouth shut.

The smell of coffee and sausage made its way to her nose making her hungry enough to put any uneasiness behind her. Not bothering this morning with her appearance, she went down to see what awaited her today.

The table, set for two, was the same, the menu of pancakes and sausage was a little change from yesterday's pancakes and bacon, so what was Frank beaming about? Her eyes went back to the centerpiece. In the middle of the table, propped up by the salt and peppershakers, was a big thick book.

Frank's eyes urged her to pick it up, so she did. It was a recipe book. Puzzled, Sarah looked at him for an explanation. Because she obviously hadn't understood, he proceeded to tell her that he felt they needed an activity, besides pruning, that they could do together. Opening the book to where he had stuck a bookmark, he showed her the recipe they would make for dinner. Sarah showed surprise, thanked him, and just like the rosebush incident, she swallowed hard and kept her mouth shut. Her mouth might be shut but her eyes were open.

They ate breakfast, washed the dishes then, bundled up against the cold, headed out to the vineyards for another day of pruning.

SAMMY WATCHED SARAH out of the corner of his eye. Pulling something over on her wasn't going to be as easy as he first thought. She didn't say much but he could almost hear her mind working. There was no way she could handle this vineyard by herself. Maybe that explained why it had been so easy to talk her into taking him home with her the night that she rescued him. He stopped pruning when a thought hit him. He had plans to use Sarah, but what if Sarah had plans to use him?

Later, they cooked dinner together. He had brought from town all the ingredients needed to make the recipe for chicken baked in a sauce of honey and pineapple. Served over brown rice, their dinner was as good as any you could order at a five star restaurant.

Bedtime found them at ease around each other. Parting to go to their separate rooms, the pat on the shoulder one night that had turned into a full body hug the next night, which escalated into a quick peck on Sarah's cheek last night, exploded into a quick kiss on the lips tonight.

CHAPTER 10

IT WAS NOON WHEN Clarence and Albert parked their stolen bikes behind the garage and approached the house. They had waited patiently down the block and watched as the family of four packed their station wagon and drove away.

Finding the right house had been easy; there were only two Cross addresses listed in the phone book. The first one they rode by had an Allen Real Estate sign in the yard.

"I hit the nail on the head the first time!" exclaimed Albert, proud that his little plan was working out.

Clarence's forehead creased. "Now you have a nail in your head? I'm still havin' trouble with your ears."

"Clarence, have you spent your life under a rock?"

"I spent most of my life in and out of jail, and I ain't never seen no rocks there."

Albert just shook his head.

Not wanting the neighbors to see them, they stayed in the backyard with cover from neatly trimmed bushes to hide them as they jimmied a window; Albert crawled in. Chubby Clarence was stuck halfway through and stayed there until Albert managed to wriggle him free.

The house had all the comforts the two had been dreaming about. The hot water ran out while Clarence was finishing his shower because Albert had stayed under the spray too long. Muttering curses under his breath, he found Albert in the big bedroom going through the walk-in closet where one side was filled with men's clothing.

"Let's get rid of our prison garb," he said, motioning for Clarence to look through the clothes. Albert didn't have a problem finding a new outfit but there was nothing in the closet that would fit short, plump Clarence. "Try the boy's room," Albert said. "You might have better luck there."

Clarence emerged from the boy's room dressed in what looked like a martial arts outfit. The white pants were too short and a bit of skin peeked over the top of his black socks. The long jacket, held shut by a rope-like tie, exaggerated his round belly.

Albert laughed. "Who are you now? Friar Tuck?"

"You're hurtin' my feelin's again, Albert!"

"Couldn't you find anythin' else that fits?"

"Do you think I'd be wearin' this if I could?"

"Well," Albert reasoned, "anythin' is better than that prison stuff."

"You promised food, Albert. I'm hungry."

"Let's go see what's in the refrigerator. If the family plans to be gone for any length of time, I don't imagine we'll find much in there."

"So what'll we eat then? You promised!" Clarence whined. "You said we'd eat."

"There's bound to be a pantry with canned food," Albert replied as he headed toward the kitchen. "A bowl of soup would taste pretty good right now!"

Indeed, the refrigerator was stripped of anything perishable, but the pantry was loaded with cans of tuna, soup, vegetables, and boxes of crackers.

"Wow!" exclaimed Clarence. "We can live here for a long time!"

Albert didn't answer. He'd found an opener and was busy eating tuna out of the can.

"Tomato soup would taste good," mused Clarence, "but I like it hot."

"Well, just put it in the microwave," Albert instructed. He was busy looking into another cabinet when a noise caused him to whirl around in time to see sparks fly as the microwave door blew open.

"Clarence, what the hell are you doin'?" he shouted.

"You said to put the tomato soup in the microwave so I did," Clarence gasped, his voice shaking.

"You idiot! You can't put metal in a microwave!"

"Well, why didn't you say so? That was pretty scary!"

"Were you raised in a barn, Clarence?"

"There you go again, sayin' bad things to me! You aren't bein' nice, Albert."

"Find somethin' else to eat, and be quick about it," Albert said sharply. "I'm tired and I want to go sleep in a real bed. I'm goin' there right after I eat this can of pineapple."

Clarence had his head stuck between shelves trying to reach a can that was way in the back. He had lined up rows of them trying to decide which one to open first.

"Baked beans! Look what I found, Albert!" he cried as he pulled his head out of the cabinet. "Mom used to make these for me!"

He was scraping the very last bean out of the can when a noise from another part of the house startled them. The faint rattling of a key and the opening and closing of a door was not supposed to be happening. The family couldn't be home this soon! A high-pitched voice called, "Simon! Where's my pretty kitty-kitty?"

Grabbing a full laundry basket, Albert dumped the dirty clothes. "Clarence." he whispered. "Quick! Help me shove this mess into the basket."

"Are we gonna get caught, Albert?" whimpered Clarence. "Are we goin' back to jail?"

"Not if we can find the door into the garage before the cat person finds us."

"I think it's that door right behind you."

"Good thinkin', Clarence! Come on! She's almost to this part of the house!"

Clarence grabbed the basket that now contained some half-empty cans, the full ones he had lined up, two spoons and an opener. They were pulling the door shut behind them just as the cat-caller rounded the corner.

"Simon, is that you I hear? Are you hiding from me again? Here, kitty-kitty! I couldn't wait to give you a special treat!"

Inside the dark garage the two men tried to calm themselves. "That was too close! I guess we didn't find out everythin' we needed to know in that office," Albert whispered.

"Yeah," Clarence whispered back. "That lady should have mentioned the cat."

"Well, now we know. Just as soon as the cat-feeder leaves we can go back inside and enjoy the house. Man, it's dark in here!"

"It's still daytime, ain't it, Albert?"

"I think it's about two in the afternoon, but since I can't see my watch, that's a guess."

Clarence was silent for a moment, and then asked, "Then shouldn't there be some light in here?"

Trying to peer through the darkness, Albert looked around. "There doesn't seem to be a window in here and the garage door fits so tight there's no light comin' in that way. But that's not a problem. We'll be back inside in a minute."

They waited patiently until they heard the faint noise of the front door closing.

"Time to go back in!" gleefully chortled Clarence.

Albert felt around trying to find the doorknob in the dark. He found it, turned it, and then muttered, "Oh, shit!"

"You said a bad word, Albert!"

"Oh shit, shit, shit, shit!"
"Quit sayin' bad words and open the door!"
"Clarence, my little pain in the ass, the door is locked."
"Shit!"

CHAPTER 11

THE SILENCE WAS DEAFENING.

"Albert," whispered Clarence, "I'm scared."

"Be quiet. I'm thinkin'."

"Is thinkin' gonna get us out of here?"

"I have no idea how to get us out of here, but I know we have to survive until that happens. Do you remember what ended up in the laundry basket?"

Clarence could hear Albert talking but he couldn't see him. "Well, I was linin' up the cans, puttin' my favorites in one row, and my almost favorites in another row, and my…."

"Clarence, just the number," Albert sounded impatient. "How many full cans do we have?"

"I can't see, but I can feel! One, two, three, f…."

"Count to yourself."

"Don't be so bossy, Albert! Four, five, six…."

"Clarence, just push the basket over here!"

"Where's here? I can't see you."

"Push the basket toward my voice."

After the sound of the basket scraping over the cement floor, Albert cleared his voice and reported. "All right. I count twelve full cans, three half full, one can opener, and two spoons."

"Did we do good?"

"It depends," Albert answered quietly. "It all depends on how long we have to stay here."

"It's getting' really cold, Albert. I wish I had my prison clothes back!"

"I guess changin' clothes wasn't such a smart idea."

"I had a little flashlight on a key chain in my pants pocket. Wish I had it now!"

"There must be light switches out here, probably around the door. Clarence, you stay here by the basket so if I get lost in the dark I can follow your voice back. So don't you move."

"I ain't movin'."

Albert cautiously prowled around. He muttered a curse when he bumped into a big smooth object that, upon examination, had a handle.

"I think I found a refrigerator," he called back to Clarence. "A light should come on when I open the door!"

"So open it!"

Clarence heard the door open. "Where's the light, Albert?"

"Remember your little mishap with the microwave?"

"Remember it? I'm still shakin'!"

"Well, you blew a fuse."

"There you go, talkin' dirty again!"

"Cl…! Oh, never mind. I'm talkin' about the electrical wiring of the house."

Silence.

"Can't you fix it?"

"No, little buddy, I can't fix it."

Silence.

"So, what's in the refrigerator?"

"I can feel cans of some sort. Guess I'll have to open one and see what's in it." After pulling the tab on the top, he put the open can to his nose and inhaled deeply. "Well, we ain't gonna die of thirst, that's for sure! There's enough beer in here for a party!"

"I ain't had a beer since before we got sent to prison. Bring over as many as you can carry! Oh, but while you're there, check and see if the refrigerator has a freezer."

"You ain't cold enough? You want some ice?"

"Just check. Mom used to keep ice cream treats in the garage freezer."

"Good thought. Humm. There are little wrapped squares of somethin' here."

"Rip off the paper and taste it."

"Hey, little buddy, you're right! It's ice cream bars covered with chocolate!"

"Can you carry some over here?"

"Since the freezer ain't workin' no more, we're gonna have to eat them before they melt."

"Bring them on! You can get the beer later. Anyhow, beer and ice cream don't go together so good."

Albert carried the box of ice cream treats across the garage using the sound of Clarence's voice to guide him. "Where should we put these?"

"In our bellies! The quicker we eat them, the less mess there'll be. How many are there?" It was too dark to see, but Albert bet Clarence was jumping up and down.

"At least four."

There was silence as the eating frenzy progressed. "Ouch!" Clarence yelled.

"Ouch? You hurt?"

"I have a pain in the middle of my forehead! Feels like a knife."

"You're eatin' ice cream too fast. Slow down!"

"And now I'm really cold! You can have what's left of my share. I've had enough." Clarence's teeth were chattering.

Albert was gathering up the garbage. "I need to find a box or something to put junk in. If we're gonna be here for a few days we don't need to live like pigs. Stay put. I'm gonna do some more explorin'."

Clarence hugged himself, trying to conserve his body heat. He listened as Albert felt his way around the walls of the garage, looking for anything that would help them. There was a clatter, a curse, and then Albert called, "Little buddy, I found a bicycle!"

"Yeah, a lot of good it will do! The people come home, open the garage door, and the two of us jump on that one bike and ride away. I don't think so, Albert. I think we're goin' back to jail."

"It would be a good replacement for your pink girlie bike, but you're probably right," he sighed, "we're goin' back to jail. Now we have to figure out how to survive until that happens."

Clarence sat in the dark, listening to Albert's noisy progress. After a crash and a muttered curse, Albert yelled, "Hey! I just fell over a stack of newspapers!"

Clarence snorted. "You plannin' on readin'?"

"No, silly!" Albert shoved a pile of papers in Clarence's direction. "Newspapers are good insulation. Fold them up and put them under your clothes. They'll hold in your body heat."

"Where did you learn that, Albert?"

"I spent one winter on the streets," he replied.

"Go on! You're pullin' my leg."

"Damn straight I did! I lived under a bridge with a few other guys. That's where Sammy found me."

"So tell me how to do this newspaper thing, and when we get warm, you can tell me stories about you and Sammy."

"Are you asking for bedtime stories, Clarence? I'm supposed to entertain you until you fall asleep? Who do you think I am? Your mother?"

"Don't yell at me, Albert. I'm cold and scared. The least thing you can do is be nice to me since we're stuck together!"

There was a moment of silence. Clarence heard Albert's voice shake when he replied, "Sorry, little buddy. I'm scared, too!"

Clarence whimpered. If Albert, his protector, was scared, then their situation was truly awful.

Changing the subject, Albert instructed. "Now listen-up. The first thing we do is to make a bed out of a pile of papers. The cement floor is cold so you want a big layer between you and the floor. Then you put many layers of paper together and stick them inside your clothes…."

CHAPTER 12

TRYING TO KEEP HER hands busy and her face straight, Clara dusted the nameplate on her desk that established the fact that she was Clara Clark, Realtor. She didn't dare look up. Until the door closed, she held back the laughter.

When she finally saw her ex, his head down, walk past the window on the way to his car, she let it all out. She had never believed that old saying that a good belly laugh was as good as sex but she just found out that if it was not, it was a good second!

She dried her eyes and blew her nose, realizing that it was truly over. No longer was there even a vestige of feeling left from her many years married to that man. As a new bubble of laughter was building up again inside her, she felt light-headed with relief.

At first, when she had looked up and seen who was coming in the door of Allen Real Estate, her heart did a little flutter. For years she had obsessed over the fact that he and his bimbo were living in her house.

After smiling sweetly, her ex laid the morning paper on her desk. She had already seen the front-page picture of herself accepting the Realtor of the Year award at the annual dinner last night, but she pretended surprise and thanked him for bringing it in. Since the two of them hadn't had an actual conversation in years, she was puzzled why her winning an award would bring him into her office.

It didn't take long to find out. He wanted sympathy! He was reaching out to Clara because his bimbo was cheating on him. This man, who had taken away her dignity, her house, her dreams, and her feeling of self worth, was here in her office because he wanted sympathy. She listened to his tale of woe while muttering words of comfort like, “How could she treat you that way?” and “How awful for you”. Inwardly she was cheering for the bimbo.

Clara tried to pull herself together because Joe and Lucky were dropping in for a visit this morning. However, just looking at herself in the bathroom mirror brought on another burst of laughter. Tears had removed the mascara from her eyes but it was easy to see where it had gone; she had black rivulets of it running down her face. This sent her into another spasm of giggles. She was scrubbing her face when the door opened and she heard the click of Lucky’s claws on the floor as he searched for her. Sticking her head out of the bathroom, she yelled a cheery “Good Morning, Joe and Lucky!”

These two had become the most important part of her life. She mightn’t have been so sure of that before the visit from her ex, but now she could look at Joe knowing that her heart was empty of old feelings.

“GOOD MORNING, JOE and Lucky!” a voice called from somewhere inside the office. Lucky and Joe looked around and then spotted Clara’s pretty face poking out of the bathroom. Joe waved hello as Lucky pulled the leash out of his hand and rushed toward her. She laughed in protest as he plastered her with kisses. When she came out of the bathroom and looked at Joe, he saw that something was different about her. She looked lighter, somehow. The Clara that walked out of that bathroom, even minus makeup, was not the Clara that Joe had met last November when she hired him to put signs in the front yards of houses she had listed. That Clara was quite rumpled, chubby, and unhappy. The day the dog scratched on her office door was the day that started the big changes in her life. The Clara that stood before Joe now, ready to take a walk with him and Lucky, was trim and beautifully dressed with a touch of blonde highlights and a new haircut. But it was the essence of Clara that was different. It intrigued Joe.

Today he was trying to stay busy enough to keep him from thinking about his two boys. His ex, Brenda, decided when he was worthy enough to spend time with them. He had been late bringing them back the last time he had them, and since she was always looking for ways to keep the kids from him, she had used that as an excuse to cancel his visit today.

Clara took Joe's arm. When Lucky worked his way between them, a feeling of contentment slowly built up inside of him.

He liked where he was right now.

CHAPTER 13

"PSSST…YOU ASLEEP, CLARENCE?"

"Not any more!"

"Sorry about that!" Albert sniffed. "I smell somethin'."

"What's it smell like? Somethin' good?"

"No, somethin' dead," Albert said. "Can't you smell it?"

"Uh, …."

"What?"

"Remember that can of beans I ate right before the cat-feeder came?"

"What are you tryin' to say, Clarence?"

"Ah, I need…."

"Spit it out, Clarence!"

"I need to go potty!" Clarence whispered.

"Oh, for God's sake!"

"But I do! What are we gonna do about…you know?"

Silence

Albert sighed. "Dump the cans of food and take the laundry basket way out there someplace. And take some newspaper with you."

"What am I goin' to do with the newspaper?"

"Clarence, do you see any toilet paper layin' around? Do I have to explain everythin'?"

"How far away should I take the basket?"

"We have to be able to find it again in the dark," reasoned Albert, "so count your steps."

"One, two, three, four…do I take baby steps or giant steps?"

"Wherever you are now, that's far enough."

"Ahhhhh!" Clarence sighed in relief.

"Holy Mother of God,!" yelled Albert. "Move the basket further back!"

Clarence grunted. "Can I wait till I'm finished?"

"You're goin' to be the death of me before this is all over!"

"Albert?"

"What?"

"How many steps did I take?" Clarence's voice came out of the darkness. "I need to come back."

"Just follow my voice."

"Albert?"

"What now?"

"I need to wash my hands."

"This ain't the Hilton Hotel, in case you hadn't noticed."

"Beer. That's it, I'll wash my hands with beer!"

"Just do it," Albert answered in a disgusted voice. "Wonder if it's day or night?"

"I heard the cat-feeder leavin' so it must be day. Don't make no difference in here though."

"One way out of here would be to pound on the door when she's here. Trouble is she probably would be too scared to open the door." Albert sounded dejected. "She'd call the cops for sure."

"But what are we goin' to do when the garage door opens when the family comes home?" Clarence wondered. "Do you think we can run out of here fast enough to get away? Our bikes are in the back. I can't ride very fast on my pink one, though."

"Let's be quiet and try to sleep."

"I'm not sleepy, Albert!"

"It makes the time go faster if you sleep."

"Tell me a story," Clarence pleaded. "Tell me about you and Sammy livin' under the bridge."

"Sammy didn't live under the bridge. I said he *found* me under the bridge."

"Don't matter. I just want a Sammy story. Please, Albert?"

Silence.

"What are you doin', Albert?"

"Makin' ear plugs."

"Out of what?"

"Newspaper."

"Why are you makin' ear plugs?"

"To shut out the sound of your voice!"

"Ah, Albert , there you go again!"

Even through the earplugs, the sound of Clarence's quiet sobs disturbed Albert. Although he didn't know anything about Clarence's background, Albert figured that life had not been kind to him.

"Little buddy," he said quietly, "I don't know any stories, or I'd tell you one. I'm scared too, you know."

Clarence gulped back a sob, "How do I always end up like this? I never meant to be a bad man. It just happened."

Albert thought about this for a bit, "You talk about your mother a lot. Is she out there somewhere worryin' about you?"

"My mother is dead," Clarence said flatly. "She died when I was ten years old."

"Who raised you then?"

"I was a ward of the court so no one raised me. I just kept gettin' moved around from family to family."

It was quiet for so long Albert thought Clarence was asleep. He rolled over, pulled the newspapers over his shoulders, and closed his eyes. Visions of his own mother appeared in his mind and a streak of homesickness hit him hard. He pictured her in church, singing, her face radiant. The song started first in his head, then into the darkness he sang. The strains of 'Abide With Me' were the comforting sounds that Clarence heard as he fell asleep.

Albert's face was wet with tears by the time he sent the last note of the song into the darkness.

CHAPTER 14

SARAH AWOKE AND braced herself for the hateful sound of the alarm. Shaking her head to clear the fog of lingering sleep, she remembered she hadn't set the alarm. There was no need to get up early today. The last row of vines had been pruned yesterday just before dinnertime. She smiled as she remembered the celebration dinner they had cooked together last night.

Frank seemed to be investing in more than just her vineyard. In one of his trips into town, he had bought one of those slow cookers. He had found a recipe in that new cookbook that he wanted to try. While they were finishing the last rows of vines, a pork roast was slowly cooking in Sarah's kitchen. She had to admit that when they walked into the house, knowing that they were done pruning for the year, the smell of that roasting pork was a celebration in itself.

Snuggling down into the warm nest of her covers, Sarah decided to wait until she smelled coffee brewing downstairs.

Much later, she woke up to silence; no good smells were coming from the kitchen. Wasting no time, she threw on some clothes and rushed downstairs. There was no sign of Frank. It didn't look as if he had made himself a cup of coffee. She looked for a note, but there was none. After starting the coffee, she reached into the cupboard for the bottle that contained her vitamin pills. Her hand came out empty. Strange. And then she saw the bottle on the shelf below. Puzzled, she opened the bottle, took out a pill, and then put the bottle back on the shelf where it belonged. She must not have been thinking yesterday morning when she put the bottle back in the wrong place.

While fixing herself a bowl of cold cereal, Sarah planned her day. Housework had been put on the back burner for weeks. Her eyes took in the clutter, dust, and actual dirt in her house. Someone had to tackle the job, and since she knew that someone was her, Sarah sighed, put down her cup of coffee, and went to the closet where all the cleaning equipment was stored. No rest for the wicked. She had no recollection of being wicked recently, and the thought made her smile as she pulled the vacuum cleaner out of the closet and went to work.

SAMMY WAS FEELING SMUG. Right now, Sarah was upstairs, waiting to smell what he was cooking for breakfast. Surprise, surprise, Sarah, no breakfast for you this morning!

Since he didn't hear her moving around, it was a good chance to check out those pills he saw her take every morning. If he was going to become the sole owner of this place, he had to start planning on how he was going to do it. Finding the pills to be capsules that pulled apart, he smiled.

He set out for town in the old work truck. This time, the trip he was making was without fear that anyone would recognize him. His beard had come in quite nicely, sunglasses covered his blue eyes, his hair looked like a gray bird's nest, his potbelly had grown, and his beautiful white smile was gone. Getting that smile back would be the first thing he would do after he got rid of Sarah.

He needed to find where she bought the chemicals that were sprayed on the vines. Asking too many questions at the wrong store was not a good idea. After the nasty deed of getting rid of her was finished, he didn't want anything to be tracked back to him. He needed to take his time. He was surprised when he realized that he was actually enjoying some of the time spent with Hovering Sarah. An unfamiliar feeling of contentment had overwhelmed him when they cooked those dinners together.

It was almost as if they were a family.

CHAPTER 15

"ALBERT, WHERE ARE YOU? I can't feel you!"

"I've been workin' on the lock. If I had my pickin' tools, I'd have us back in the house in three minutes."

"Could we break the door down?"

"Can't. It's solid."

"Solid what?"

"Just solid! Take my word for it, Clarence; we ain't breakin' down that door."

"How about the garage door?" Clarence wasn't about to give up.

"What about it?"

"We know it works; we saw it close when the family drove away."

"There's a garage door opener somewhere, but I can't find it. It must be in the house. I don't know how you would open the door manually. While you were sleeping, I've been feelin' my way around. I didn't find nothin'. Damn, it's dark in here!"

Silence.

"How many days do you think we've been in here?"

Albert sighed. "I don't know. Based on the times I heard the cat-feeder come and go, I'd say about four days."

"There aren't that many cans left. What happens to us then?"

"I guess we'll get really hungry! But as long as we have something to drink, we should last for a long time."

"I'm hungry right now," Clarence said. "Are you?"

"I had a can of green beans while you was asleep. So open a can. On the way back, I'm stoppin' at the refrigerator. We need more beer."

"You've been really drinkin' a lot of that stuff, Albert."

"Why not? Nothin' else to do!"

"Oh! Wanna guess what's in the can I'm opening?"

"Don't want to."

"Albert, you're no fun!"

"So, all right. I just hope it's not a can of beans."

"Ah, shoot! This shouldn't count!"

"Why not?"

"It's just broth. I think it's chicken broth."

"Rules are rules. So drink it slow, because that's your ration for the day."

Clarence listened to the rustling of Albert's paper bed and the sound of beer cans being set down on the cement floor. "Clarence, why don't you fill up on beer like I intend to do?"

"I don't want no beer, thank you, but I'd like a story! Please tell me a story, Albert! Or sing to me! I hate it here in the dark when you go to sleep."

"Little buddy, I'm puttin' in my ear plugs and I'm gonna drink myself to sleep. No stories, no talkin', no singin'. Understand?"

Silence.

Clarence hunched his body under the layers of newspaper and listened in pitch-blackness as Albert dropped empty beer cans onto the cement floor. One last burp, a rustle of papers, and then complete silence.

The sound of someone sobbing shook Clarence out of the dark despair that had settled over him. Feeling his cheeks, he was surprised to find tears running down his face. How had this all happened? His life was a nightmare that didn't seem to have an ending. He needed to move, to do something other than to lie here and listen to Albert's drunken snore.

He made his way cautiously, using his nose and counting his steps to the basket, where he relieved himself. Since Albert was always the one who did the exploring, Clarence had no idea what lay out there in the darkness. He decided to find out; anything was better than doing nothing.

With both arms extended in front of him, he cautiously took baby steps into the darkness. Catching his foot on the knocked-over bicycle, his body pitched forward into a free-fall. His flaying arms encountered a wall and, with relief, he reached out his hands to steady himself. One hand landed on something cold and round. Clarence caught his breath. He'd found a doorknob!

In disbelief, Clarence turned the knob and the door opened. He stepped out of absolute blackness into a world of blue skies, white clouds, and sunshine!

"Albert! Wake up!" he shouted. "We're outta here!"

Hearing the unmistakable sounds of the garage door opening, he whirled around. From down the block, he saw a car slowing down and making the turn into the driveway.

"Albert!" Clarence yelled. "For God's sake! Wake up!"

Albert didn't move. Clarence, knowing it was now or never. ran around to the back where they had hidden the bikes. The sounds of yelling voices coming from the garage told him they had found Albert, lots of empty cans and a smelly laundry basket.

Hiding behind the bushes, he stuck around long enough to see a drunken Albert with crumpled newspapers hanging out of his clothes, hug one of the cops as they led him to the squad car.

Picking up Albert's bike, Clarence rode away.

CHAPTER 16

"HEY, MITCH! WAIT UP!"

Detective Mitch Hatch looked behind him and saw his police officer brother-in-law heading in his direction. "What's up, Tom? You look like the cat that ate the canary!"

"Sometimes things just drop into your lap, kinda like a gift from heaven." Tom was grinning.

"Uh, Tom, you don't strike me as someone who has a direct link to heavenly gifts," Mitch laughed.

"Wait till you hear this!" Tom exclaimed. "You know the Crosses over on Hill Street? Well, they were gone for a few days, and when they came back, they found a guy sleeping in their garage!"

Mitch looked puzzled. "If the family wasn't there, why would a guy live in the garage when there was a perfectly good house available?"

"He'd locked himself out of the house! For some reason he went into the garage, shut the door behind him, and then found he couldn't get back into the house. The garage has no window in the access door, and I checked for myself. It is absolutely pitch-black in there."

"How do they know he was in the house to begin with?" asked Mitch.

"There's evidence that he used the shower," answered Tom. "Now here's is something we haven't figured out yet, and the guy isn't talking. There were two piles of dirty clothes on the bathroom floor, proof that there were two of them. They evidently helped themselves to clean clothes because Mr. Cross recognized the outfit the guy had on; it was his. Remember those two I saw in the restaurant the other day?"

"I didn't pay too much attention to them," Mitch recalled, "but you did."

"For some reason, they looked familiar to me. I'm pretty sure the guy in jail right now is one of them."

"So, where is the other one?"

"That's the mystery." Tom shook his head. "The garage has two piles of bedding made out of newspapers, and the amount of food that was consumed in the few days the Crosses were gone points to more than one person. I'm not even going to mention about the deposits left in the laundry basket…."

"Thanks for sparing me!" Mitch laughed. "So you're thinking that both of those men you saw in the restaurant were living in that garage."

"Makes sense," answered Tom. "The one in jail seems to be as puzzled as we are when we ask about the other guy. Unless he is one heck of an actor, he really doesn't know where his buddy is. But we're pretty sure both of them were in there together, we just haven't figured out why his buddy left him behind when he found the access door."

"Why did they take food with them when they went into the garage?"

"The Crosses figured that out. Their next-door neighbor went in every day to look after the cat. Why she went in the day they left was a mystery until she explained she had bought some special treats for Simon and couldn't wait to give them to him. There's a pile of the family's dirty laundry that used to be in the laundry basket. They think the two were eating when the cat-feeder entered the house. Not wanting to leave a mess that would make her suspicious, they scooped everything into the basket and took it with them when they ducked into the garage. Can you imagine how surprised they were when the door locked behind them?"

"How many days were they in there?" asked Mitch.

"The Crosses were gone for four days."

"That would be a long time to spend in complete darkness," Mitch said quietly. "Cold, too."

"The guy had lined his clothes with newspapers! The cops that picked him up are still laughing. I guess he was quite a sight when they hauled him away."

"It's a good thing the family hadn't gone on a long vacation. Wonder how long they would have survived in there."

"They had found that the garage refrigerator was stocked with beer, so there was no danger of them dying of thirst. In fact, the guy was quite drunk when the Crosses came home and called the cops," Tom chuckled. "It was such a relief to be rescued that he cried and hugged the cops all the way back to the station."

"But where is the other guy?"

"When we figure that one out," Tom said, "I'll tell you!"

"So who is the one you have?"

Tom shrugged. "He's not talking, but his fingerprints are being checked against the ones we have on file in the double murders in McGuire's Alley. Two of Sammy the Grunt's gang members didn't get out of jail when Sammy did, but prison records show that they're out now. We think they came here looking for Sammy."

"Maybe they'll have better luck because we sure haven't found him!" Mitch sighed.

"If we could just find his car! I can't believe with all the agencies looking for him, no one has come up with the slightest idea of where he went."

"So what's the guy in jail saying?" Mitch inquired.

"Aside from muttering obscenities about his absent buddy who got out and left him behind," Tom chuckled, "he's not talking."

"Keep me up to date on this, Tom. Looking for Sammy is at the top of the things I'm investigating. He stabbed you, and he threatened my wife with a knife. I have a personal interest in finding him."

"I'd like to get my licks too!" Tom said. "Too bad I wasn't a better shot."

"The fact that you even got a shot off after he stabbed you is surprising enough," Mitch said firmly. "Asking you to aim better is a little much!"

"I know. It was just a shoulder wound, according to Molly, who, unfortunately, saw it up close. By the way, how are my sister and my favorite niece and nephew?"

"We're all fine except for lack of sleep," Mitch replied. "I walk around like a zombie most of the time. Those feedings in the middle of the night are brutal."

"I thought you had hired what's-her-name to help," said Tom. "I thought she was supposed to make life easier for you and Molly."

"Her name is Anita. She's really good with Kim and Laurie, and that helps a lot."

"When you took custody of your brother's kids when he and his wife were killed, I thought you had bitten off more than you could chew. But you made it work, and I applaud you for that," Tom patted Mitch on the back.

"Those two girls love the twins…almost too much," laughed Mitch. "I went from being a lonely bachelor to being a busy family man in the matter of a few years. Who knew?"

"Does taking care of Kim and Laurie take up all of Anita's time, or does she help with the twins, too?"

"Big time! I don't think Molly could handle them all by herself. Anita offers every night to put the bassinets in her room, and I wish she would! Molly, so far, has refused."

"If she gets tired enough, maybe she'll change her mind. For your sake, I hope she does! But I have to go," Tom said. "I'm meeting Marie at the hospital on her lunch break."

"How are things going with the two of you?"

"Better than I have the right to expect! Remember when I came out of the coma after Sammy stabbed me, and I saw Marie for the first time? I thought I had died and she was an angel. The family is still teasing me about that. But I was right the first time."

"You're telling me after all these months, Marie hasn't done anything that would make you clip her angel wings?" Mitch sounded dubious.

"My feet haven't come down from the clouds yet," grinned Tom "I can't believe she's wearing my ring."

"Have you two set a date?"

"Nothing in stone." Tom sighed, and then added, "We're just enjoying the moment."

"I wish for you and Marie the same happiness that I have with your sister," Mitch said, and with a half smile, he confided, "Molly and I have something very special."

"Yeah, buddy, and remember you almost wrecked it!" Tom's voice wasn't friendly.

"That's all behind us now, Tom. I'd like to forget about it, if you don't mind."

"There are some things you shouldn't forget, Mitch. Her restless legs are under control now, but what if the medication stops working? I hear it happens." Tom stepped closer to Mitch. "Are you going to remember what you learned when she was pregnant and couldn't take her 'magic' pills, as she calls them?"

"When and if that happens, I'm sure you'll remind me," Mitch replied, tight lipped.

"You can count on it! She's my sister, and I love her. I don't want to see her go through again what she did the last time when she couldn't use the medication!"

"I said drop the subject, Tom!" Mitch was angry.

"All right, I'm dropping the subject!"

"And, while you're at it," Mitch said coldly, "you can keep those accusing eyes to yourself, too."

"Mitch, these aren't accusing eyes," Tom replied quietly. "They're just watchful eyes. Bye."

CHAPTER 17

SAMMY WAS WAITING FOR the traffic light to change when his attention was drawn to two men who were standing on the sidewalk having a heated discussion. His interest was intensified when the one wearing the police officer's uniform turned his head and Sammy was looking into the green eyes of the snitch, the one that had sent him and his two what-used-to-be best buddies to jail. The snitch was supposed to be dead. Sammy shook his head in disgust. He had aimed for the heart, but not only had he missed the target, the snitch had been able to get off one lucky shot. Sammy rubbed his still-aching shoulder.

So intent was Sammy's attention on the snitch that he shut out the sound of horns blaring behind him. It was only after the green-eyed snitch glanced over to see what the racket was all about that Sammy snapped out of the trance. He was pretty sure his appearance had changed so much that no one would recognize him, but why push his luck?

He found a parking spot for the old work truck and pulled the list from his pocket. Sarah's instructions were to look around and establish which stores had the things on the list. They had found some of the items in catalogs but Sarah wanted to compare prices before she made the purchases. The list included netting, liquid soap, pump guns, smudge pots, replacement parts for the frost-protection sprinklers, and the chemical Bordeaux. He was only interested in the chemical. From the books he was reading, he knew Bordeaux was sprayed on the vines to protect them against mildew and other diseases. Somehow, he would find how he could use it in his plan to get rid of Sarah.

Walking with his head down toward the hardware store, he almost missed seeing the back of a man who was standing holding up his bicycle and peering into the window of the coffee shop. Dressed in what looked like an ill-fitting martial arts outfit, the man's reflection showed he had several days' worth of whiskers on his unshaven face. With a start, Sammy realized he was looking at Clarence. Determined to get the upper hand before Albert appeared, he jammed a stiffened finger into Clarence's back.

"Move, and you're dead!"

Clarence didn't move. In the window, he could see the reflection of a man he didn't recognize.

"Mister," his voice quivered, "if this is your bike, just take it!"

"Down on your luck, Clarence?"

"You know me?" squeaked Clarence. "Who are you?"

"I'm your worst nightmare. Where's Albert?"

Clarence croaked, "How do you know Albert?"

"Ah, come on Clarence," Sammy laughed. "You tellin' me you don't recognize your old buddy?"

"Sammy! Oh, God! Am I glad to see you!" The bike clattered when it hit the cement and Clarence threw both freed arms around Sammy.

"Whoa! What the hell's goin' on? I thought you and Albert was plannin' to do bad things to me!" He pulled Clarence's arms away.

"What did you expect we would do when we found the box almost empty?" Clarence cried. "That wasn't fair, what you did, Sammy!"

"So where is Albert?" Sammy asked, looking around. "Is he gonna come runnin' around the corner and hug me, too?"

"Albert ain't comin' around no corner. He's in jail."

"Back in jail, eh?" Sammy lifted an eyebrow. "Want to go into the coffee shop and tell me about it?"

"I'd best not go in that shop. Albert and I stiffed them the last time we was there," Clarence confessed. "But I'm *so* hungry!"

"Wait here. I'll order somethin' to go. We can sit on that bench over there and you can tell me your story."

"Sammy," pleaded Clarence. "Bring back lots! I ain't eaten in days."

"Ah, the story's gettin' better!" chuckled Sammy. "I'll be back! Don't move."

Clarence pulled the jacket of his martial arts outfit close to his body. He was shivering, not just from the cold, but also from fear. Sammy wasn't someone who would put up with fools and, as Albert was always pointing out, that's what Clarence was. He was looking around for a newspaper in the trash when Sammy returned.

"Whatcha lookin' for?" Sammy asked as he removed food from the paper sack and placed it on the bench.

"A newspaper."

"You a reader?" Sammy sounded surprised.

"No. Albert showed me how you taught him to keep warm by usin' newspapers."

Sammy let out a short laugh. "When did he say I taught him that?"

"When you found him livin' under a bridge."

Sammy snorted. "The gutter didn't look like no bridge to me!"

Clarence looked confused. "You found him in the gutter?"

"That's where his old gang threw him after they beat him and left him for dead," answered Sammy.

Clarence's mouth dropped open in surprise. "So Albert's tellin' me stories?"

"Probably," Sammy grinned. "Does it matter now?"

"He never told me about gettin' kicked out of no gang."

"Well," Sammy commented, "there are some things that guys keep to themselves."

Clarence thought for a moment. "He musta done somethin' really bad!"

"There's gang rules, Clarence. Albert broke a gang rule."

Clarence shook his head. "I ain't never heard of no gang rules."

Sammy knew the answer to the question, but he asked it anyway. "Did you ever have a woman, Clarence?"

"Can't say that I have."

"But what if you did have a woman and one of your buddies took her away from you?"

"Guess I'd want to hurt him," Clarence answered quietly. "Is that what happened to Albert?"

"Yes," Sammy answered. "Albert is a good-lookin' man. There's somethin' about him that draws women to him, so I can't say that it's entirely his fault. Didn't matter if it was a girlfriend, a wife, or just one of those women who like hangin' around badass men, word is he bedded them all. But what finally got him beat up and left in the gutter was when he was found in bed with the leader's wife."

Clarence thought for a moment. "So the rule is not to mess with someone else's woman?"

"That's it, and don't forget it."

"Well, he's in jail so it don't matter now," Clarence reckoned. "Can I eat?"

"Eat one sandwich and then stop," instructed Sammy. "You can have the second one when you finish your story."

Making short work of the sandwich and the soft drink, Clarence mopped his face, and started to talk. Sammy listened in disbelief. Stiffing restaurants, a failed apple snatching, and stealing a free book was funny enough, but Clarence's colorful account of the four days spent in the pitch-black garage had him holding his sides.

Sammy's laughter was making Clarence incensed. "You think it's funny, Sammy? You don't see me laughin'!"

"Tell me again how you got out." Sammy blew his nose and wiped his eyes. "I ain't laughed this hard in a long time!"

"I feel like punchin' you in the nose, Sammy!" Clarence was close to tears. "It ain't funny!"

"So they hauled old drunk Albert off to jail and you rode away on his bike. Want to check back to see if the little pink girlie-bike is still there?" Sammy doubled over again.

"Can I have the second sandwich now? Please? All we had to eat was one can of something a day, but it was hard to know when it was another day. Sometimes we would hear the cat-feeder come in and that helped us mark time."

"Finish it all, Clarence. I'm sorry I laughed so hard. Guess it was partly in relief that it wasn't me who was stuck in the garage for four days."

"Where you livin', Sammy?"

"Let's start with this. I ain't Sammy no more."

"You ain't Sammy?" Clarence was shocked. "Then who are you?"

"My name is Frank Adams."

"Who the hell is Frank Adams?" Clarence asked, looking confused.

"It's a long story, Clarence."

"Well, the story I just told you wasn't short! So come on."

"The stolen ID I had in my pocket when I had a car accident said I was Frank Adams from Detroit. The lady who stopped to help me kept callin' me Frank and I didn't know who she was talkin' to." Sammy thought for a bit, then added quietly, "Could've been funny, but it wasn't."

"You still haven't said where you're livin'. And why do you look so different?"

"Because I'm hidin'! The whole town is lookin' for Sammy the Grunt. I did some bad stuff and I can't afford to have them find out who the handyman at a local vineyard really is."

"You did really bad stuff?" Clarence asked with an expectant look on his face. "Bad like Albert?"

"No, not like Albert," Sammy shook his head. "Things just happened and I had to do what I did."

"Like what?"

"If you call offin' a real estate agent on her lunch hour and stabbin' a local policeman bad, then, yeah, I did some bad stuff," he answered.

"Wow! But now you're a handyman at a vineyard? They feed you there?".

Sammy laughed and rubbed his stomach. "Haven't you seen my potbelly?"

"Do they need more help at the vineyard? I really need to find a place to hide because Albert is *so* mad at me. He hasn't figured how I got out and why I left him there to be found."

"How do you know that?" questioned Sammy.

"I heard two guys talkin' about it."

"Was one of them a policeman?"

"Yeah," Clarence nodded his head. "I seen him before in the coffee shop and he looks familiar. He has red hair."

"There's a reason he looks familiar. Remember that kid in the gang that we called Zeek?"

"Yeah. You made fun of him all the time," Clarence laughed.

"I should've done more than make fun of him," Sammy grumbled. "He was a snitch!"

"So who'd he snitch on?"

"Dummy, he was workin' undercover for the police," Sammy said indignantly. "Remember I said I'd stabbed a cop? He's the cop and he should be dead, but he's not! Pisses me off. He got lucky and shot me in the shoulder."

"He shot you?" Clarence's eyes were wide.

"Sure did! I'll tell you about it sometime. But what happened to the clothes they gave you when they let you out? I'm sure they didn't push you out of jail into the real world in that outfit!" Sammy started to laugh.

"Cut that out, Sammy!" Clarence's face was turning red. "You're makin' me mad again!"

"Well, answer my question," Sammy said, trying to keep a straight face.

"After we had our shower in that house we broke into, Albert said we should get rid of our prison clothes. He had no trouble findin' somethin' that fit him, but I had to go to the boy's room to look. Nothin' fit but this thing. What is it anyway?"

"It's some kind of outfit you wear when you do karate."

"Albert called me Friar Tuck. Does Friar Tuck do karate?"

Sammy was off again, holding his sides.

"Clarence, you're good for me. You make me laugh. Grab your bike and let's put it in the back of the pickup truck. I'm takin' you home with me. On the way there, we can come up with a good story to tell Sarah."

"I ain't good at makin' up stories. Albert always did that."

"But now you have me and you're in better hands. Trust me."

CHAPTER 18

SARAH WAS PUZZLED ABOUT why she had such an empty feeling when Frank went into town today. While she didn't trust him, just having him around was better than nothing. The house was so quiet. After Larry's death, she had gone through periods when she didn't even want to live because of the loneliness. However, eventually she had gotten over it and had actually started to appreciate the feeling of independence when the Frank thing happened.

The house was just starting to smell good. Frank had put a chicken in the slow cooker before he left for town. She was walking though her recently cleaned house, enjoying the fact that she had a good dinner to look forward to, when she heard the truck pull into the driveway. The surprised but pleasant feelings she had from Frank's return abruptly vanished when she looked out the window and saw that he wasn't alone. The door opened on the passenger side and a short chunky person in some kind of white outfit got out. Sarah went to the door to greet them.

"Frank?" She had a question in her voice. "You brought a visitor?"

"Sarah, it's a long story, but say hello to Clarence."

Without looking her in the eye, the short chubby man in the strange outfit took Sarah's outstretched hand.

Turning to Frank, she said, "Try me. I like long stories."

"Well." Frank looked at Clarence for help. "When I first noticed him, he was lookin' in the window of the coffee shop. He was hungry but he had no money for food, so I took pity on him and bought him lunch. Turns out he flew into town and the airlines lost his luggage."

Sarah looked at Clarence. The outfit he was wearing didn't fit him. The pants were too short, and she saw bare skin peeking between where his black socks stopped and his pant legs began.

"Uh, Clarence, I assume you arrived in town dressed like this for a reason?"

Before Clarence could answer, Frank chimed in with, "He's a karate instructor."

This man was no more a karate instructor than Sarah was the Queen of Sheba. For one thing, he smelled. His hair was greasy and he hadn't shaved for several days. She tried to look Frank in the eye, but that didn't work either. These two were up to something.

Frank sniffed. "That chicken sure smells good! Clarence is goin' to stay for dinner, if you don't mind." With that, he pushed the man further into the room and gave her a big smile. So, Sarah guessed, they had a guest for dinner, whether she minded or not.

Together they worked in the kitchen to put the finishing touches on the meal. The strange little man set the table and helped with the cleanup after dessert. She was wondering when Frank was planning to take Clarence back to town when he informed her that Clarence was going spend the night.

"Is the airline trying to find the lost luggage?" Sarah asked hopefully.

"They sure are! Clarence called the airline and they know to send it out here when they find it. They assured him that someone from the airport would personally deliver it."

The rest of the evening was strained. She pulled Frank aside and whispered. "That man smells. I don't care what your story is or why you brought him home, but he's not crawling into one of my beds until he showers."

Frank tried to get a hurt look on his face at the mere suggestion that Sarah wasn't swallowing his story. When that didn't work, he nodded his head.

"I thought that since he might be here for a few days waitin' on his luggage," and here Frank had the grace to blush, "he could help us in the vineyards."

The plot thickens.

"In those clothes?"

"I'm thinkin' maybe we could find somethin' for him to wear while he's waitin'."

"Good luck! Some of Larry's old work clothes are still in the laundry closet, but they won't fit Clarence. Neither will any of yours."

"There're some clothes down in the shed left behind by the workers last harvest season. I'll go get them. Think we could run them through the washer and dryer tonight?" he asked.

"I'm not part of that 'we', Frank. If you want to do it, go right ahead. I'm going to bed."

And she did.

SAMMY FROWNED. That didn't go so well. Smart little Sarah was suspicious. The story he had made up about bringing Clarence home was a weak one, but then, so was Clarence. What choice did he have? Sammy couldn't afford to have him hanging around town and being picked up by the cops. Clarence could tell them that he knew where to find Sammy the Grunt; that would be a great bargaining chip. Now, if jailed Albert kept his mouth shut, this whole affair would soon blow over.

Sammy had some clean clothes ready for Clarence by the time he'd showered, shaved, and was ready for bed. Clarence was almost silly with excitement. His last night in jail was the last time he'd slept in a bed.

Sarah had not made a sound since she went off to bed. Tomorrow morning was going to be interesting.

CHAPTER 19

SARAH DIDN'T WAIT FOR the alarm to go off. She wanted to be down in her kitchen, cooking her own breakfast before Frank and Clarence made an appearance. Frank had taken over running her life, her vineyard, and her home. For a while, it had been almost a relief to have someone to lean on, and she had been content to let him do it. Well, no more. Sarah was taking back what was hers.

By the time she finished cooking a pot of oatmeal, she heard them whispering together at the top of the stairs. Frank didn't look too happy when he stepped into the kitchen and found her cooking.

"I promised Clarence pancakes and bacon," he complained.

"Well, that's not what he's getting," she muttered as she plopped oatmeal into three bowls. Clarence, feeling the tension in the kitchen, scuttled to a seat on the far side of the table.

"At least we should have toast, don't you think?" Frank asked.

"There's the toaster. Help yourself," Sarah replied shortly.

Frank was getting the picture. "So what are your plans for us today?" he asked.

"Today we start tying up the shoots. I'll have to show you and Clarence how to do it." She looked over at Clarence huddled over his bowl of oatmeal. He was dressed in a collection of clothes that was almost as ridiculous as the martial arts outfit he had arrived in yesterday, but the clothes were clean, and he looked clean, too. Frank hadn't been shaving his own face, but he must have loaned his razor to Clarence.

After a silent breakfast, neither man offered to lend a hand in clearing the table or doing the dishes. There were good and bad things in the old arrangement with Frank, so if she was going to make changes, she guessed she couldn't complain when the good things changed. No one said a word until she was finished. Sarah had so aggressively attacked the pots and pans the kitchen hadn't been completely silent.

From the cupboard she took out the package of twisty-ties and the three of them bundled up and headed for the vineyards. Spring had finally arrived and things were growing. The sun was shining down on their backs and, after a cold winter, it felt good.

They gathered around while Sarah showed them how to look for shoots that needed to be attached to the wire, using the twisty ties. Larry liked to leave about ten shoots on one plant or at least enough of them to meet the shoots on the next vine. It didn't take a rocket scientist to do this, but the next step was tricky. She glanced back at Clarence who was watching her closely. Why Frank brought him home last night was a big puzzle, but he seemed willing enough to work. She just didn't know how bright he was. The next step, if not done correctly, would kill her vines.

Carefully, Sarah showed them how, when you moved the shoot to wrap it, you gently bent it enough to hear a little crack. Too much bending and the shoots snap in two. Larry never told her what was the technical terminology or the theory behind this activity, but it had something to do with stimulating the energy flow into the shoot. She supposed she could look it up in one of the books that Frank had lying around. Maybe Frank already knew, but under the new management, he wasn't talking.

Sarah straightened up and started to walk out of the vineyard.

"You goin' somewhere?" Frank called.

"I'm going into town for supplies," she called back over her shoulder.

"I thought we was gonna do that together!"

"You went into town yesterday to check prices, but all you came back with was Clarence."

"You gonna be gone long?" he yelled at her back.

"Long as I have to be," she shot back, not looking around.

He hollered, "But what about dinner?"

"What about it?"

"I thought we'd do somethin' out of the new cookbook," he whined.

"So do it."

Sarah continued her brisk walk toward the house. Her head was high and so was her determination to take back her vineyard.

She could feel Frank's eyes on her as she walked away. He was probably wondering how badly he had messed up his little plan of wooing her. All the good things, the breakfasts, the one rose, the fudge, the cookbook, the slow cooker, and all those rose bushes were negated by one Clarence.

Since she hadn't been in town for months, she went back into the house and took a long, hard look at herself in the mirror. The face she was looking at in the mirror suddenly assumed a determined expression, and she realized that she had come to a decision. Grabbing the yellow pages, she found the number of a beauty shop; her fingers dialed before she could change her mind. Running upstairs, she changed clothes and applied make-up to a face that hadn't seen such care since Larry died.

CHAPTER 20

THE CHURCH LADY WAS ecstatic. In all the years that she had obeyed God's command to be a missionary to the unfortunate inmates in the town's jail, she had never run into such a find as the one in there now. She blushed as she put the finishing touches on what she had chosen to wear today. The man always commented on how nice she looked, and she couldn't wait to hear what he'd say about her new hat.

The man could sing like an angel! Their voices blended when they sang "The Old Rugged Cross", and when he closed his eyes and threw back his head to hit the high notes, The Church Lady truly felt the hand of God. She had no idea what the man was accused of, but in her mind and she was sure in God's mind too, the man was a saint.

ALBERT SAT IN HIS CELL wondering what the hell he was going to do. He could hear voices coming from the front office but he couldn't always make out what they were saying. He did hear that the FBI had his fingerprints so he knew it was just a matter of time before they found out who he was. He had to get out of here, but how? If he couldn't find his way out of a garage that had an access door for anyone who was bright enough to find it, how the hell was he going to get out of jail?

He could hear the Church Lady coming towards his cell. When she wasn't around, he made fun of her, but secretly he enjoyed her visits. Something that was making a remembered noise was coming along with the Church Lady. Along with two deputies, Albert could see she was pushing a piano. Unbidden thoughts fought against years of carefully built barriers, but the familiar jangling sound of a piano being moved jogged those memories.

IN THE SMALL TOWN where he and his mother had lived, the church was the center of everything. It had an assembly room that was open every day of the week for any organization that wanted to use it. Albert's mom was a joiner, and several times a week she dragged him with her to a meeting, stuck him in a side room, told him to be quiet and wait for her.

The room had a piano.

When Albert had told Clarence, "Let's play it by ear" while hatching the plan to get access to a phone book, it had not occurred to him that he really did have the ability to play by ear. The hours spent waiting for his mother in that room were the happiest hours of his childhood. He figured out melodies with one finger, found what other notes sounded good with that note, and so built chords that pleased his ears. When he mastered how to play 'Happy Birthday' in one key, he worked until he could play it in all keys. In time, any tune he could hear, Albert could play. Finding and watching professional pianists became an obsession. When he was back in that side room, he would duplicate, improvise, and improve on what he had observed.

It wasn't until his mom heard God's calling and started to haul him to church services within driving distance, that his talent was revealed.

The two had traveled to a nearby town where signs had advertised the coming of a revival meeting featuring a well-known singing evangelist. The tent was filled with people who had come with high expectations, but the meeting deteriorated when the starting time came and nothing happened. Finally, a spokesperson appeared and apologized, saying that the person who traveled with the evangelist and accompanied him on the piano had fallen ill. A groan went up from the packed audience; they had been looking forward to gospel music.

Albert's mother was astounded and embarrassed when her son got up and marched down the aisle towards the front.

"I can play!" the quiet crowd heard the young lad tell the spokesperson.

To his mother's utter surprise, he played.

The evangelist and his audience loved the added attraction of such a young musician, and eventually he talked Albert's mother into allowing the boy to accompany the group during the summer months. This was Albert's life until, at age nineteen, it ended.

He had listened to many sermons about the evil of lust. He had been doing quite well suppressing his strong attraction to the opposite sex, but earlier that day he had used his charm on the fifteen-year-old daughter of the choir leader. He had talked her into doing things that were frowned upon by the law, the evangelist and, of course, the girl's father. During the altar call, when the evangelist was urging all sinners to come to the front to pray for forgiveness, Albert saw the girl talking to her dad and pointing to him at the piano. He was playing soft back-up music to the altar call when he saw them moving in his direction. The full offering plates had been placed beside the piano for later counting. Without even planning it, Albert grabbed the top plate, lifted up a tent flap, and disappeared into the night.

ALBERT SHOOK HIS head to get rid of the unbidden memories, and back to his immediate problem.

Last week, the Church Lady had said she wished they had a piano to help with the music. One of the guards spoke up and informed her that there was a piano in the community room.

"But who can play it?" she had asked.

"I can play," Albert had called out from his cell.

Albert raised his eyes as the Church Lady and the piano paused in front of his cell. "We're going to have some fun!" she chortled.

There had been several other inmates, but all had been discharged earlier in the day. Albert was the only prisoner in the jail and the only one in the whole building who could play the piano.

"Please, could you let this nice man out of his cell? It would be just for a short while, just long enough for a few songs. What could it hurt?" The feathers on the Church Lady's hat quivered.

To tell the truth, the two guards had been enjoying the duets the Church Lady was singing with the prisoner. Once, when he threw his head back and sang with his eyes closed, they saw a tear running down his cheeks. No one wanted to talk about the day, when at the end of 'Amazing Grace', there was not one dry eye in the whole building. The guards looked at each other, shrugged, and unlocked the cell door.

Albert couldn't believe his luck. Somehow, he had to use this opportunity. There probably wouldn't be another one before the FBI got back to this hick town with their findings.

He hadn't touched the keys on a piano for years, but his fingers hadn't forgotten. Never before had such music filled the town's jail. He closed his eyes and imagined himself once again under the tent with the singing evangelist. Old hymns he hadn't thought of in years came to life as his fingers danced over the keys. The guards and the Church Lady listened in utter amazement. He finally opened his eyes, remembered where he was, and switched to the first line of a familiar song. The guards and the Church Lady were singing a rousing "Jesus Loves Me", when they became aware of loud voices coming from the front office. Someone yelled back to them, "They found the car!"

Reacting to the news, the guards turned and started for the front, better to hear the details.

Albert realized it was now or never. “Sorry about this,” he muttered to the Church Lady as he reached up, grabbed her hat, pulled it down over her eyes, and smashed her head into the piano. The crash of her head hitting the keys was not a melodic sound.

He looked for the nearest exit and used it.

CHAPTER 21

SARAH HAD MADE HER HAIR appointment the last thing on her list. By the time she pulled into an empty parking place right outside the beauty shop, the bed of the old pickup truck was full of supplies for the vineyard.

The shop was packed with women and the chatter was lively. Listening to the laughter in the women's voices, Sarah became aware of how starved she had been for human contact. She was thinking that she had to do this more often and not isolate herself out on the vineyard, when the door flew open and a pretty woman burst into the shop.

"They found Sammy's car!" the woman yelled.

All activity in the shop came to a halt.

"Where?" asked Betty, the beautician who was cutting Sarah's hair.

"Remember that scenic lookout on 116? The place where Eileen's body was found? That's where the car was found, wrapped around a tree."

"Was Sammy in the car?" asked the brunette who was getting a permanent.

"No, but there are blood stains. Animals have lived in the car all winter and nested in the upholstery, but so far there's no sign of what happened to Sammy."

"That accident happened last November. If Sammy did manage to get out of the car alive, I would imagine someone will find what's left of his body this summer," commented the woman who had taken her head out from under the dryer.

"Who is this Sammy?" Sarah asked Betty, who had started cutting again.

"Sammy the Grunt. Can you imagine someone with that name? I guess it's his gang name. Anyhow, he caused quite a stir last fall. He broke into a house, murdered a real estate agent named Eileen, stabbed a cop, got shot, and disappeared. Nothing quite so exciting has happened in our town before or since Sammy."

"And this happened last November?"

"Remember that bad snowstorm? That's when it happened."

"What does Sammy look like?" Sarah asked, afraid to hear the answer.

"Hey, Clara! Want to tell Sarah what Sammy looks like?" yelled Betty, waving her scissors.

Clara, the pretty woman who had brought the news to the shop, blushed. "Are you going to tease me about the crush I had on him?"

"Why not?" laughed one of the ladies.

"Sammy *is* beautiful. I had every right to have a crush on him!"

"Would you please describe him?" Sarah asked quietly.

"He looks like a god. There isn't a spare ounce of fat on him, his smile is brilliant, and he smells good, too."

"That doesn't describe anything. What color is his hair?"

"Blond."

"You say he was shot?"

"The cop he stabbed? Well, Tom got off one lucky shot before he passed out."

"Where was Sammy shot? I mean what part of his body?"

"The shoulder."

"How bad is this Sammy?"

"I don't think you'd want to meet him in a dark alley!"

The girls laughed.

Sarah was between the growing feelings of dread and fear. Not want to meet him in a dark alley? How about sleeping under the same roof?

She looked at her image in the mirror. Her dark hair had been cut short, blown dry, and it framed her face like a cloud. Betty, her beautician, was telling her how easy her hair would be to care for now, but Sarah wasn't listening. The police station was right across the street. She had to tell them. She had to run over there right now and tell them where they would find Sammy the Grunt. They would find him out in her vineyard with a strange little man who appeared out of nowhere yesterday.

She threw two twenty-dollar bills on the counter and ran out of the shop.

CHAPTER 22

ALBERT BOLTED OUT OF the side door of the jail and frantically looked around. A pickup truck parked across the street caught his eye. The bed of the truck was full of supplies of some kind and, seeing nowhere else to hide, he dived for safety under them. Covering his body with what looked like a bolt of netting, he curled up in a fetal position and held his breath. He could hear all hell breaking loose across the street at the jail. Sirens screaming and the shriek of brakes announced the arrival of an ambulance. He cringed. He had really liked the Church Lady. Hearing rapidly approaching footsteps, he held his breath. Whoever it was paused briefly by the truck and then proceeded to run across the street. He let out his breath and squirmed further under the netting.

SARAH RAN OUT OF THE beauty shop, paused by her truck, then crossed the street to the jail. She stood inside the door and tried to get someone's attention. Finding Sammy's car was no longer the top issue. An escaped prisoner and something about a Church Lady, whoever that was, had eclipsed that news. No one was staffing the front desk. In the middle of all the commotion, an ambulance pulled up and attendants in white disappeared into the back, only to reappear a bit later carrying a stretcher with a body on it. A red feather was poking out from under the blanket.

Frantically she tried to get someone's attention, but no one noticed her. Police, running from the station in pursuit of the escaped prisoner, pushed her out the door.

Finding herself back on the sidewalk, she turned and made her way to the truck. How could she go back to the vineyard knowing that Frank was not really who he said he was? Was she sure? Some of the description fit, but not completely. But how many injured men would be out on the road on a snowy November night by the lookout on 116? Just one, she had to admit, and she had picked him up and taken him home out of desperation. To Larry's memory, she murmured, "I'm sorry."

She drove home slowly, not really wanting to get there. Should she turn around and go back to the police station? If she didn't go back, what was she going to do? Just pretend she didn't know anything? Just go along with Frank as if she believed him? He was a good worker; what would she do for help in the vineyard if she lost him? How dangerous was he to her? Would he really hurt her?

THE UNINVITED HITCHHIKER, dressed in the jail-issued orange outfit, was apprehensive, too. How he would handle the situation that awaited him when the truck stopped was the big question.

The sound of crunching gravel and the slowing down of the truck chased away the memory of the Church Lady. He lay as still as he could when he heard voices of two men calling greetings to the driver. A woman's voice answered them. As the greeters got closer, Albert couldn't believe that he was hearing his garage buddy Clarence, and his old gang leader, Sammy! What the hell was going on?

The lady wasn't too enthusiastic with her greeting to the two men. She just quietly asked for their help in unloading the pickup, and then Albert heard crunching gravel as she walked away.

"Think she's still mad at us?" Albert recognized Clarence's voice.

"Ah, she's got a bug up her arse about somethin'. She'll get over it." Sammy answered. "Take hold of the netting on your side, and let's get it out first."

They had made the decision for him.

With the netting removed, Sammy and Clarence were shocked and amazed to see Albert struggle to his feet and jump over the side of the truck

The three of them stood rigid.

Albert couldn't believe his luck. The truck that he had sought refuge in had taken him to the two people he needed to find. Clarence, who was staring at him with his mouth hanging open, had some explaining to do, and Sammy, if it really was Sammy, had to account for the missing money. Now was not the time to settle old scores; now was the time he needed the help of friends, good or bad.

"Sammy, is that you? You sound like Sammy but you sure don't look like him!" Albert finally broke the tension.

"This is the new me, so get used to it, Albert. Now would you please tell us what the hell is goin' on?"

"Bad stuff is goin' on! I need to hide!"

"What kind of bad stuff have you done now, Albert? Messin' with the ladies again?" Clarence smirked.

Albert angrily grabbed his arm. "You have a lot of explaining to do, buddy! There better be a good reason why you left me in the garage, but I'll settle that with you later, you can count on it!" He turned to Sammy. "The trouble I'm in now has nothin' to do with messin' with somebody's lady."

"Then, what?" questioned Sammy.

"I kinda hurt the Church Lady when I escaped from jail."

"The Church Lady? So it *was* lady trouble!" Sammy said sarcastically. "Ain't you ever gonna learn?"

Clarence was frantically trying to get their attention. “Sarah’s comin’! Move!” he whispered as he pushed Albert towards the tool shed.

“Run, Albert!” urged Sammy. “Don’t let her see you! We’ll talk later.”

Sarah walked up to the two men who had done nothing about unloading the truck. “Were you waiting for me to tell you where to put the supplies?” Now that she knew who the man she had been calling Frank really was, she avoided looking at him. How good an actor was she?

“Ah, yes, actually.”

“We’ll just pile them into the tool shed. I’ll move some stuff in there to make room,” she said as she headed in the direction of the shed.

“No need, Miss Sarah.” Running to the shed, Clarence blocked the doorway with his body. “Me and Frank can handle this. You’re lookin’ far too pretty to dirty your hands on bags of fertilizer! Don’t she look pretty, Frank?”

“Clarence is right for once, Sarah! You sure are lookin’ good! Why don’t you let us do the dirty work today?”

Sarah hesitated, then backed away. “Frank, what’s in the slow cooker? It smells wonderful.”

“Corned beef!”

“So it’s corned beef and cabbage for dinner?”

“That’s right!”

Sarah pondered as she walked away. Maybe she could learn to live with the situation. Maybe, if she kept her mouth shut, things would stay the same. But what would happen if the man found out she knew who he really was? If he truly was someone you “don’t want to meet in a dark alley”, how safe should she feel sleeping in the room next to his?

She stepped into the warm house that was filled with the wonderful smell of corned beef. Without Frank’s help, her vines would grow out of control and her vineyard would be worthless in a few years. How dangerous was he to her? She certainly wasn't a threat to him. Maybe nothing bad would happen if she played along with him and pretended the trip into town hadn't changed anything. That was it; hear nothing, see nothing, and say nothing. It was better to have him than not to have him. Having arrived at a decision, she smiled to herself and began setting the table for dinner.

CHAPTER 23

SAMMY SLIPPED OUT OF the quiet house and made his way toward the shed. The night was black without the slightest hint of a moon; using a flashlight was out of the question. Walking on the grass instead of the gravel path muffled the sound of his steps. Because the darkness made familiar shapes look strange and disoriented him, he walked into the side of the shed.

Albert, hiding inside feeling deserted and hungry, heard a bump followed by a muttered, "Damn!"

"I sure hope that's you, Sammy!" Albert whispered.

Finding the door, Sammy opened it and went into the shed. "Man, I can't see a thing! Where are you?" He jumped as Albert's hand touched him.

"I've had it with dark places!" Albert complained.

"Don't see that you have much to say about the situation, Albert. What would you have done if the truck you stole a ride in took you someplace else?"

"You're right. That was one lucky choice I made, crawlin' into Sarah's truck! But I sure am hungry. Did you bring anything' to eat?"

"Yes, but how we gonna do this? I can't even see where to set this stuff down."

"What else did you bring?"

"Clothes. You have to get rid of that orange outfit you're wearin'. I brought you some stuff that was in the laundry closet. I think they belonged to her dead husband. They're clean."

“So, what’s the plan?” Albert asked as he groped in the dark for the food that he could smell but couldn’t see.

“You’re gonna have to wait until dawn so you can see what you’re doin’. You have to dump that orange jail suit, but for God’s sake, don’t hide it here in the shed!”

“Think I’m dumb enough to do that, Sammy?”

“Don’t push me, Albert. I’ve heard of some of the things you done before I picked you out of the gutter.”

“Drop it, Sammy.” Albert’s voice was cold.

“Albert, do you really think you’re in any position to tell me what to drop? I can’t hear your head shakin’, but the answer to that question is ‘no’.” Sammy’s voice was deadly quiet.

“All right, I get it. Just tell me what to do and I’ll do it.”

“At early light you will leave here, walk toward the main road, and wait there until you see some activity around here. You will then walk down the driveway, introduce yourself to whoever is out, and claim you are down on your luck and need a job. You have from now until then to come up with a good story. Sarah needs workers but she doesn’t have the money to hire them, so offer to work for food and a place to sleep. Sarah is not dumb; keep that in mind.”

“What name should I use?”

“Use Albert. I doubt very much if that’s your real name anyhow. But remember, my name is Frank. Mess up on that and we’re all toast.”

“I’d love to hear the story behind that!” Albert chuckled.

“Talking about stories, I haven’t heard how you managed to get out of jail.”

In pitch-black darkness, Albert picked up the story starting with what happened after Clarence escaped from the garage and his own arrest. Sammy was half listening to the story about the Church Lady and the piano. Albert got his attention when he explained that he was able to escape because the guards looked in another direction when they heard someone yelling, "They found his car!"

Sammy gasped. "Whose car? Did they say whose car they found?"

"No, but everyone seemed to know whose car they were talkin' about. Do you know? Everyone was makin' such a fuss about findin' it. Even when I was hidin' in the bed of the truck, I could hear people on the street talkin' about it."

"Where was Sarah when this was goin' on?" Sammy hissed.

"How should I know? Why don't you ask her?"

"This is bad!"

"Is it as bad as what I did to the Church Lady? Don't you want to hear about that?"

"No, I don't want to hear about what you did to the Church Lady, but since she probably was a bit older than you like 'em, I don't imagine you molested her," a disgusted Sammy replied.

"Molest her? Hell, I think I killed her!"

"Way to go, Albert." Sammy jeered. "Now you're wanted for murder, too."

Albert backed away from Sammy and changed the subject.

"So why are you so upset about a car being found?" he asked.

Sammy was quiet for a moment, and then he answered softly, "Because it's my car. I was runnin' away from the cops last November when I hit a deer and went over a cliff. That's where the car has been all these months."

"So, how did you end up out here?"

"I crawled up the hill and made it to the middle of the road. Sarah stopped, got me into the car, and brought me here to the vineyard. The identification I had in my wallet said I was Frank Adams from Detroit."

"So you've been living here with Sarah since November?"

"Yes. This arrangement might change, though, depending on what she heard in town. I hope, for her sake, she didn't hear anything."

"She seems like a nice lady. You'd hurt her?"

"Probably about as much as you hurt the Church Lady."

Albert squirmed. He had really liked singing hymns with that lady.

Sammy found Albert's hand and passed the container of leftover food. "I'm going back to the house now. Stick with the plan, come up with a good story, and I'll see you tomorrow."

"How you gonna figure out if Sarah heard about your car?"

"I don't think she's much of an actress. If she knows, she'll give it away somehow."

Stepping out of the shed into a night so dark he couldn't see his hand in front of his face, Sammy paused to get his bearings before heading in the direction of the house.

It was too dark for him to see the fluttering of a window curtain in an upstairs bedroom.

CHAPTER 24

FEELING HELPLESS AND SCARED, Sarah huddled by the window, looking out at a night so black it was impossible to see a thing. She knew Sammy wasn't the only one out there.

Who was in the shed?

She had thought she could live with the information she had picked up in town and just act as if Frank really wasn't Sammy the Grunt. Needing Clarence's help in the vineyard, she had thought she could pretend that the funny little man was indeed a lost-luggage casualty. But who was in the shed?

Dinner had gone well. Clarence and Sammy had kept up a lively and entertaining conversation. Both helped with the clearing of the table. She had felt like a lady of leisure when Clarence washed and Sammy dried. Sammy got out the card table and the three of them played poker with matchsticks until bedtime. Something funny was said as they headed to bed. When they separated to go to their rooms, they were laughing.

She could do this, she had told herself. Pretending was a game that she had been good at as a child. Those were the positive thoughts that had gone through her head as she started to drift off to sleep. That was when she heard Sammy tiptoe past her room; the squeak in the third step down on the stairs alerted her that he was up to something. Crawling out of bed, she crept halfway down the stairs. Thanks to Larry's dislike for the dark, several nightlights helped her follow Sammy. He was in the kitchen, working quietly. From the open refrigerator door light, she could see he was filling one of her plastic containers. He went into the laundry room then, with the container in his hand and a bundle of clothes under his arm, he went out.

Later, she heard the door close downstairs. Sammy was back inside. She could hear him sneaking up the stairs. When he paused by her unlocked door, she held her breath. She'd never thought she needed to lock her bedroom door. Tonight had changed everything.

Her heart was pounding and her eyes refused to stay shut. In a room down the hall, there was a man who "you don't want to meet in a dark alley". In another room, there was a child-like person who gazed at Sammy as if he were his hero. Sarah would swear that those two knew each other before Sammy picked him up in town.

Suddenly, she remembered that Clarence had stood in front of the door to the shed and wouldn't let her go in. That meant Clarence and Sammy were in this together. Whoever was in the shed was no stranger to either of them.

CHAPTER 25

SARAH WAS STILL AWAKE WHEN the alarm went off. What would happen if she pretended to be ill and just stayed in bed? Pulling the covers over her head, she tried to quell the shudders that shook her body. Larry. Her need for him hit her with a force so strong that it made her breathless. She rolled over to his side of the bed but, instead of finding warmth from his body, she felt only cold. "Larry, Larry!" she whispered. "What have I gotten myself into?"

She cried tears. This surprised her because she thought she had shed her life's allotment of them when he had died.

The smell of coffee and bacon coming from the kitchen told her that Sammy was back to cooking. Maybe she should stay up here and watch out the window to see if he sneaked breakfast to whomever was there in the shed. But no, she needed to pull herself together, go downstairs and act as if nothing had changed. They had work to do in the vineyard.

Hunger and curiosity finally got her out of bed. The image she saw in the mirror this morning startled her. That trip to the beauty shop yesterday had made quite a change, not only to her life, but also to her appearance. Even spending most of the night with her head under the covers hadn't completely ruined Betty's creation. Encouraged by what she saw in the mirror, she took a bit of care with her attire for the day, surprised that looking good made her feel stronger.

Before she headed downstairs, curiosity got the better of her. She walked back to the window, hoping to catch Sammy sneaking breakfast out to the shed.

What she saw made her gasp. Stifling a scream, she tumbled to the floor.

Larry was walking down the driveway.

SAMMY STOPPED IN THE middle of stirring pancake batter, cocked his head towards the ceiling, and listened. "I think Sarah finally got out of bed. About time! She'd better get down here pretty soon or she's gonna mess up all our plans."

"Tell me the plans again, Sammy," pleaded Clarence. "I don't wanna mess up"

"You already messed up, dumb head! You call me Sammy one more time and you're outta here!"

"Don't yell at me Samm.....Frank!" whimpered Clarence. "I'm trying!"

"Well, try harder!"

Clarence wiped his eyes. "You haven't told me the plan."

"Albert is supposed to wait until he sees activity around here and then walk down the driveway. Remember, Clarence, we don't know him. We've never seen him before. Can you handle that?"

Clarence's face crumbled. "There you go again!"

"Okay! But don't ruin the deal we got goin' here."

"What's his name?" Clarence sniffed.

"I told him to stick to Albert," said Sammy. "That probably isn't his real name anyhow."

"So what's his story?"

"Other than that he needs a job and will work for room and board, I don't know," Sammy said. "He's had all night to come up with a good one."

"It's awful quiet up there," Clarence said as he looked up at the ceiling. "Maybe she went back to bed."

"Clarence, go look outside. Albert ain't one to play by the rules. I wouldn't put it past him to make up his own."

Clarence reluctantly gave up his watch over the sizzling bacon and stuck his head out the door.

"Samm…Frank! Albert is halfway down the driveway! What do we do now?"

Sammy was in the middle of an obscene oath, describing what he was going to do to Albert for changing the rules, when a loud thump from the room upstairs stopped him in mid-tirade.

"Did you hear that?" asked Clarence.

"Of course I heard that. You think I'm deaf?"

Before Clarence could answer there was a knock on the door.

"Shit. So much for plans. Answer the door."

Clarence opened the door and saw Albert in the clothes Sammy had taken to the shed. The front of his tee shirt read, "Lovers and wine improve with age".

CHAPTER 26

SARAH HEARD VOICES. Feeling something cold on her forehead, she opened her eyes. What was she doing on the floor? Struggling to sit up, a wave of nausea hit her; she lowered herself back to the floor.

When Sarah hadn't come down for breakfast Clarence had gone up to check on her. After knocking several times, he inched the door open and saw Sarah on the floor. His yells brought Albert and Sammy running up the stairs.

"I think she musta hit her head on the dresser when she fell," she heard a strange but vaguely familiar voice say. "She has a pretty big knot back there."

"Wonder what made her fall?" That sounded like Clarence's voice.

Sarah opened her eyes, and then closed them. It wasn't a dream. Larry was here in their bedroom. He stood behind Sammy and Clarence just looking at her. He had on the shirt she had given him on his last earthly birthday. They had laughed when he put it on after she had given him his real gift, an early morning hour of love. She reached out to Larry.

"I think she wants to meet you," a puzzled Sammy said to Albert.

Albert knelt down on the floor beside Sarah.

"Larry, Larry! Please tell me this isn't a dream!" she whispered as she picked up Albert's hand, kissed it, and then placed it over her heart. Her eyes closed.

"What the hell?" exclaimed Sammy.

"Hey," yelled Clarence. "What's Albert doin' with his hand on Sarah's boob?"

"Albert, get your hand off her! If anyone's going to feel her boob, it's me!" hissed Sammy.

"What name did she call me?" Albert ignored Sammy's claim of ownership and kept his hand where it was.

"Larry. She called you Larry." Clarence answered from the other side of the room where he was looking at a collage of photographs.

"Anyone know who this Larry might be?" Albert could feel Sarah stirring.

"Larry is the name of her dead husband. This is weird," Sammy said.

"Uh, maybe it ain't so weird," Clarence was waving a picture in the air. "You gotta see this!"

The three men studied the picture Clarence had removed from the wall.

"You wanna explain this?" Sammy asked Albert.

"Explain what?" Albert squinted at the picture.

"What the hell is your picture doin' on Sarah's bedroom wall?"

"That ain't my picture! What are you talkin' about?"

"The hell it ain't! You need glasses?" Sammy hissed.

Albert pried his hand from Sarah's grasp and carried the picture to the window. How could this be? He was looking at his own face. Sammy and Clarence watched him as he ran a hand over his features, one by one. The black hair and widow's peak, the dimple in one cheek, the cleft chin, the blue eyes, and the smile were identical.

"How can this be?" he muttered.

"You sayin' that ain't you?" Sammy yelled.

"Calm down! You know very well this ain't me!"

"You have a twin, then?"

"Not that I know of."

Sarah was reaching around, searching for Albert's hand. When she didn't find it, she sat up, opened her eyes, and took in the scene. Clarence and Sammy were huddling close by and a third man was standing by the window looking at a picture. She almost fainted again when Albert turned and looked at her. "Ma'am, I'm Albert." He held out his hand to Sarah; she didn't move. She just stared.

"Ma'am?" Albert took a step towards her. "Are you all right?"

"You aren't really Larry then?" Sarah whispered.

"No, Ma'am, I ain't."

"How can this be?" she whimpered.

"I don't know." Albert shook his head.

"Then who are you?"

"Just someone down on his luck looking for work. I thought I might find a vineyard that would let me work for room and board." Albert hung his head trying to look dejected.

Sarah rubbed the knot on the back of her head. This man was not Larry, but the shock of seeing his double had lowered her guard. Things were getting sticky and she had to think clearly. This man had spent the night in the shed. Since she was convinced that Sammy and Clarence were no strangers to each other, she remembered that this third man was connected to them too. How much danger would she be in if Sammy knew she had watched him take food and clothes to the shed last night? And how was she supposed to act around a man who was the double of her dead husband?

"Sarah," Sammy broke into her thoughts, "we seen the picture of your dead husband so we know what you thought when you saw Albert. But he's just someone out of work who is lookin' for somethin' to eat and maybe a job."

Sarah stared at Albert as she rose from the floor and made her way to sit on the bed. "Would you mind coming a bit closer?"

Albert hesitated a moment before he went to Sarah. He knelt on the floor and raised his face to her. Placing a hand on each side of his head, she held it gently as her eyes devoured a copy of the face that she had loved so dearly.

"Larry's dimple was on his left cheek. Your dimple is on the right one."

"Appears so," Albert answered. The scrutiny was making him uncomfortable.

"Larry was left-handed. Are you?" she asked.

"No, Ma'am. I'm right-handed."

Sarah sighed. How was she supposed to survive living in the same house with three unsavory men who were probably up to no good? It didn't help that one looked like her dead husband. Before releasing Albert, she lowered her head and placed a soft kiss on his lips. No one was more surprised than Albert.

"I didn't kiss you, Albert. I kissed Larry. You can stay on as a worker if you will do it for room and board. Now if you will excuse me, I'd like to be alone."

The three men backed out of the room, heading for the kitchen and a cold breakfast.

Sarah locked her bedroom door.

CHAPTER 27

"MAN, THAT WAS CREEPY," muttered Albert, breaking the silence of a very subdued breakfast.

"Would someone please tell me what's goin' on?" Clarence pleaded.

Albert laughed. "I spent most of the night in that damn shed makin' up a story. That was a waste of time! Even in my wildest dreams I could never touch what went on in that bedroom upstairs."

"You sure shook up Sarah!" Sammy commented.

"I kinda liked that little kiss," Albert grinned.

"Albert, that's what I want to talk to you about."

Albert tilted his chair back. "So talk."

"From now on, if anyone is goin' to feel her boobs, it's me," Sammy informed him. "If anyone kisses her, it's me."

"You have somethin' goin' with her?" Albert looked closely at Sammy.

Sammy thought about the rose, the fudge, the cookbook and slow cooker that he had used to woo Sarah. "I've been tryin'. This vineyard is gonna be mine one of these days, and I'm not gonna let you get in the way."

"You're gonna own the vineyard? How do you plan on doin' that?"

"Marry her." Sammy smiled his toothless grin.

Albert smirked. "Have you looked in the mirror lately, Sammy?"

"Hey, watch it with that Sammy stuff! I don't know what Sarah heard in town yesterday. And yes, I've looked in the mirror."

"You didn't answer the first question," prodded Albert.

"I was workin' on the marriage angle before you showed up. But you ain't stayin' around here much longer to spoil things."

"And why is that?"

"You're a wanted man, Albert! Did you forget that little thing?"

"I ain't forgot. But I can't think of a safer place to be than right here."

"Didn't you just hear me tell you that you ain't stayin' here?"

"Because of Sarah?"

"That's a good enough reason, don't you think? Look, Albert, I know why your old gang kicked you out. You messed with their women. Sarah's mine!"

"I don't know what stories you heard, but I was innocent in some of those cases. The women wouldn't let me alone and I admit I'm only human."

"Well, I ain't givin' you a chance to be human around Sarah."

"Ah, Samm…Frank, let's you and me think about this for a minute. If you make me leave, there's a good chance the police will find me. Since I know where Sammy the Grunt lives, I just might give them that information."

Sammy's face turned livid with rage.

"Hold it! Hold it! No violence, please!" Albert threw up his hands in defense. "I'll stay away from Sarah as much as possible. The whole situation makes me feel funny anyhow."

Clarence, feeling the hostility in the air, retreated to a corner of the kitchen. "Hey, you guys, you're scarin' me!"

"Everything's fine," Albert soothed Clarence. "Samm…Frank and I need each other, and this is too good of a set-up to throw away because of a little disagreement. Right, Samm…Frank?"

"Just watch your mouth, Albert! All right. If the three of us are goin' to be here for any length of time, I need to go to town and buy clothes and supplies. I've been wearin' Larry's clothes and some of them will fit you, Albert, but I don't think that's a good thing to do. Seeing you in Larry's clothes might make Sarah faint again. Clarence needs stuff that fits, too. So make a list of things you need, and I'll go to town this mornin'. I need to hear what the people in town are sayin' about you, Albert. You said you did somethin' to a lady when you broke out of jail. Do you think you killed her?"

"God, I hope not!" Albert muttered.

"Both of you clean up the breakfast mess," Sammy ordered. "There's work to be done in the vineyard, but only if Sarah comes down and tells you what to do. I haven't heard a sound comin' from that room."

"Think I should go up and check?" asked Clarence.

"No, and your job is to keep Albert away from Sarah while I'm gone. Got that?"

"Ah, come on, I already told you I feel weird around her," Albert waved his hand. "You don't need Clarence to watch me."

Clarence and Albert, their heads together, were listing the things they wanted from town when Clarence stopped mid-sentence, whirled on Sammy and exclaimed, "Where you gonna get the money to buy us stuff, eh? From our money that was in the box?"

Albert's head jerked up. "Thank you for remindin' me! I think we promised old Sammy here that we was gonna rearrange some of his body parts when we found him!"

"Come on, guys! What's past is past." Sammy whined.

Albert whirled on him. "It's not past! You have no idea what me and Clarence went through! You caused all the bad things that happened! I can't believe that for a while I forgot that the four days in a dark garage, breakin' out of jail and maybe killin' a nice lady was entirely your fault! We got into trouble because we was tryin' to survive without any money! You stole it all!"

Clarence and Albert rushed Sammy and pinned him between the table and the wall. Albert's clenched fist was aimed at Sammy's face when from behind they heard, "Something the matter, boys?"

Albert lowered his arm and draped it around Sammy's neck. "No, ma'am, we're just horsin' around! Ain't that right, guys?"

Sarah watched the three men struggle to look innocent. "Anything left from breakfast? Coffee, maybe? I'm hungry."

"Frank is goin' into town, but Albert and me are stayin' here. Can I cook you somethin'?" Clarence asked.

"Toast. I'd like a cup of coffee and a piece of toast. After that, it's work in the vineyard. Clarence, I'm counting on you to teach Albert how to tie up the vines. Think you could do that?"

"I was good at it, Sarah!" cried Clarence. "I didn't break one stem. But Frank did. Did he tell you that?"

"No, he didn't, Clarence. That makes me glad that you're the one who is going to teach Albert."

"I'll bring somethin' back to cook in the pot for tonight's supper. Any suggestions?" Sammy asked, relieved by the reprieve from Albert and Clarence.

"How about pork and sauerkraut? Mom used to make that for me," Clarence piped up.

"Pork and sauerkraut it is then."

Grabbing both lists and the keys to the truck, Sammy escaped out the door.

CHAPTER 28

THE SLAMMING OF THE kitchen door and the sound of the old truck laboring to start was music to Sarah's ears. Having Sammy out of the house gave her a feeling of relief. Taking a deep breath, she realized she had been holding her body rigid. She was sure he was up to no good, and probably Clarence and Albert weren't choirboys either, but she wasn't having the same reaction to them. What she had heard in town about Sammy the Grunt was frightening. The man who had called her vile names and left her that Saturday was the real one. The nice one that came back that same day was the pretend one. There was no doubt in her mind now. She had brought a truly evil man home that snowy night, and now her life depended on her ability to act as if she didn't know.

"You all right, Ma'am?" Albert asked politely.

Sarah shook herself and looked into his eyes. Instantly she was transported back to the water cooler in the Birmingham law office where she, a paralegal secretary, had met Larry. Her entire body reacted to a sensation that made her gasp and reach for the back of a chair for support. Albert's expression hadn't changed, but he didn't break the connection. Clarence was saying something.

No one was listening.

SAMMY WALKED THROUGH the town with no fear that someone would recognize him. His beard had grown quite full, and he slouched as he walked. Sammy the Grunt had never slouched.

From listening to people talking in the shops, he learned that there was a statewide manhunt for both Sammy the Grunt and the escaped Albert. No one was talking about a dead lady. That was a piece of information Sammy hadn't yet decided how to use. It might be easier to keep Albert under his thumb if he thought he had killed that woman.

A display in a store window caught his eye. There on a piece of black velvet lay a vial of very expensive men's cologne. Sammy stopped and remembered. On the day he had been discharged from prison, he had splurged on this one thing. He remembered feeling wonderful that day, as if the world was his for the taking. He had looked like a god, his smile was brilliant, and great things were going to happen right after he made a little revenge visit to the people who had put him in prison. That sure had backfired! He hesitated for a brief moment before opening the door and going into the little shop. He deserved that cologne.

For the next few hours Sammy shopped. Using the lists, he bought shaving cream and razors, toothbrushes and toothpaste, combs, and working clothes. Since neither of them could leave the vineyard, he figured they didn't need any dress-up clothes. His last stop was the grocery store where he bought supplies for tonight's dinner. By this time, he was getting antsy to get back. He didn't trust Clarence to keep Albert and Sarah separated.

Sammy had no way of knowing that it was already too late.

CHAPTER 29

ACCORDING TO ALBERT, life is a series of decisions. Mess up on one, and your whole life changes.

It was bedtime and Albert could hear Clarence in the next room muttering to himself. Maybe he was praying. If Albert could remember how, he'd pray too. But trying to remember would jar loose some well-buried and painful memories. He placed the pillow over his head and recited the alphabet backwards, the states and their capitals, and half of the multiplication tables. Tonight, none of the tricks was working. Unwanted memories flooded his head.

He missed his mom. She must be worried sick about him, but he couldn't contact her. He knew someone was watching her, trying to get a lead on where he was.

There had always been just the two of them. His mom never would tell him anything about his father. Nothing. She would hug him and say that they didn't need anyone else in their lives. There was always money for everything. It wasn't until he got older that he started to wonder about the unending source of support.

You might say he was home-schooled, but it wasn't his mother who had taught him. He had a series of tutors that showed up daily. They did such a good job that he graduated from high school at age sixteen. Where did the money come from? Mom would just smile when he asked her. He entered the state's university at age seventeen and he would have started his junior year that fall if he hadn't made the one decision that wrecked it all. Messing with the choir director's underage daughter wasn't really a decision, though. It was just the reaction he had to a pretty girl who certainly looked a lot older than fifteen. The night he fled from the tent meeting, he had no idea that he was never going back. He thought he was just fleeing an angry father, but it turned out to be so much more than that.

What surprised him was that no one noticed a missing offering plate. The one he had grabbed when he ran from the tent had enough money in it to finance the next couple of weeks. At least he hadn't been branded a thief. It really bothered him that he couldn't remember that girl's name. He had ruined her life but when he thought about her, she had no name. Her Uncle Bill, who worked for an agency that had initials, was determined to punish Albert for ruining his niece's life. Their little tussle in the back of the piano-truck was short but productive. Her parents kicked her out when they found she was pregnant. That was when her Uncle Bill stepped in, placed her in an unwed mother's facility, and stood by her until she delivered and the baby was adopted.

The story got muddled after that. She never went back to her family. Her Uncle Bill tried to stay in contact with her, but even he lost her in the big city where she made a living on the streets.

At first Albert stayed in contact with his mom. She sent him money, and he thought that eventually he could resume life and finish college. Not so. Uncle Bill was determined to find him and make him pay for what he had done. That was when Albert stumbled onto the protection offered by a gang. He embellished the story of being sought by a group with initials. He didn't tell them why he was being hunted, but the initials evidently impressed the leader because the next thing he knew, he was declared a member in good standing. He had trouble when the gang did objectionable things, such as the double murder in McGuire's Alley, but he mostly bluffed his way with tough talk and little action. He was sent to prison for murder, but Sammy was the one who had done the killing. Appointing himself to be the lookout, he and Clarence had been far away from the scene when it happened. Clarence, to Albert's knowledge, had never hurt a living thing his whole life. He was just a simple little man who hung out with the wrong crowd.

So here he was, a wanted man, maybe even a murderer, living under the roof of a nice woman who thought he was her dead husband. Weird. How long could he hide here? And what was that strange current that felt like electricity when Sarah and he stared into each other's eyes? Sammy had her staked out as his own. Was he going to have more trouble over a woman?

The bed was firm, the pillow was soft, and for a brief moment, he felt safe.

CHAPTER 30

MARIE SPOTTED TOM at a back table in the hospital cafeteria. All decked out in his police uniform, it was easy to pick him out in a sea of white-coated medical workers. His red hair, freckled face, and green eyes were hard to miss, too. She knew, from past experiences that the expression on his face, when he spied her, would be that of a boy when he first saw the puppy under the Christmas tree.

He pushed back his chair, stood up, and welcomed Marie with his 'I got my puppy!' beaming face. "I thought lunch hour would never get here!" he murmured, burying his face in her hair.

"Missed breakfast again?" teased Marie.

"Silly, you know what I mean! I was hungry for the sight of you." His eyes took in the vision of his fiancée, all six feet of her. Even in her nurse's uniform, she managed to look like a model.

"Well, I'm here now so what are you going to do about it?"

"I'm going to devour you with my eyes while I eat my lunch. Did you notice what the specials are today?"

"That's a laugh! A hospital cafeteria with specials? I don't think so."

Tom drank in the sight of her smiling face. His family was still teasing him about his thinking she was an angel when he came out of the coma, but he figured he had the last laugh. That angel was wearing his ring, a reality that amazed and humbled him.

After walking through the food line and filling their plates, they returned to the table. "Anything interesting going on in your part of the hospital?" Tom asked.

"Not since they brought in Ida Tucker," Marie replied.

"How is the Church Lady?"

"Angry and disillusioned. I'd say she is having a religious crisis."

"How's that?" He raised his red eyebrows.

"She was so taken with the prisoner! I guess the two of them sang up a storm, and she thought she had brought him back to God. She claimed only a man without sin could sing and play the piano the way he did. Now she is even questioning the existence of a God that would let something like this happen."

"That's going a bit far, don't you think? How badly did he hurt her?"

"She has a big lump on her head from being slammed into the piano, but the hat protected her from getting really hurt. She claims he apologized to her before he did it."

"That was the good Christian thing to do," Tom chuckled.

"Have you found out who he is? And weren't there two of them?"

"We had enough fingerprints from the house and garage to figure it out. They are two of Sammy the Grunt's gang members who went to prison for the McGuire's Alley murders. Sammy just got out of prison earlier than they did. We think they came here looking for him."

"Looks like they can't find Sammy either. But at least you found his car," Marie remarked as she rearranged the food on her plate.

"I can't believe that the two of them have disappeared. I saw them in the coffee shop together the other day. They looked familiar, and I couldn't for the life of me figure out where I had seen them before."

"Did you ever figure it out?" Marie asked.

"Remember, I was a plant in Sammy's gang."

Marie cringed.

"Those two hung around Sammy like flies on a turd," Tom said as he scraped his empty plate. "Clara and Joe met them, too."

"I heard they stole bikes from the kids' playground."

"They did. They were riding them past Allen Real Estate when Joe and Lucky stepped out of the office, causing an accident. Joe took them in to clean them up and Clara fed them coffee and brownies. That's where they picked up the idea of living in the Cross house while the family went away for a few days. They listened to Clara's conversation on the phone with Mrs. Cross."

"Isn't it strange that real estate keeps cropping up into most all of the crimes committed recently in our little town?"

Tom thought a bit. "You're right. Sammy used the lockbox to gain entrance into that one house and he hung out at real estate offices listening for information and flirting with the secretaries. Clara had a huge crush on him."

"Don't forget poor Eileen Miller. He killed her on her lunch hour. At least he didn't treat her first to lunch at the hospital," Marie observed as she picked at a lump of gray-colored mystery meat. "And then there was that open house that brought it all to a head." Marie shuddered, reached out her hand, and touched Tom. "That's when I almost lost you before I even found you."

Tom took her hand and squeezed it while looking longingly at the food she hadn't eaten.

"If it took nearly dying to meet you, I don't regret getting stabbed by Sammy. I only wish my aim had been better when I got that one shot before I passed out."

"Getting one shot off was amazing! And you did hit him in the shoulder. Don't forget that," Marie remarked as she slid the uneaten portion of her lunch over to Tom.

"Do you remember the final clue that made Clara figure out that the good-looking man everyone was looking for was Sammy?" asked Tom between bites.

"Smell," answered Marie. "The woman at the open house was describing the man who had come into the house with her. It was a general description that could apply to a lot of men, but when she added the fact that the man smelled good, Clara put the pieces of the puzzle together and realized it was Sammy."

"Wonder what made him smell so good."

"Probably some expensive cologne. You had better not use anything like that! How could you sneak up on criminals if they smelled you coming?"

The two of them were laughing when Detective Mitch Hatch approached their table. "Whatever you two are smoking, I want some. I need to laugh!"

"Life getting you down, Mitch?" asked Tom. "My sister treating you badly, I hope?"

Mitch pulled up a chair and sat down. "Eh, it's not so bad. Sleeping is highly overrated anyway." He yawned and rubbed his bloodshot eyes.

"Mitch, you look awful!" Marie observed.

"Thanks. You sure know how to make a man feel good." His eyes drooped.

"How's Molly holding up? Does she look as bad as you?" asked Marie.

"I don't see too much of her, to tell you the truth. The twins have her attention most of the time during the day, and at night, well, she's back to her old walking habits. I don't think her pills are working their magic anymore."

"Sounds like she needs to go back to Dr. Parker."

"She did. He has her on a combination of several drugs now. I found her wandering around the dark house the other night. She was so disoriented she didn't know where she was."

"That's awful!" exclaimed Tom. "Molly has been plagued with this strange leg thing all her life. When she thought she was the only one in the world who had this problem, she didn't share her symptoms with anyone. She had been told so often that nothing was wrong with her legs, therefore the problem was in her head. The best thing that happened after she met Dr. Parker was finding out the condition has a name and that there are millions of other people in the world who suffer with the same problem. Just knowing she was not alone was such a relief!"

"May I ask what you are doing here at the hospital? And don't tell me you came here to eat the food." Marie pointed to the gray glob that even Tom hadn't eaten.

"I'm here to talk to Ida Tucker. I've tried for the past several days, but the good woman was so hysterical she didn't make sense."

"Do you really think she has information that will help you find the escaped prisoner? I heard the two of them just sang together. And who, pray tell, gave the guards permission to let him out of the cell to play the piano?" Tom's red eyebrows were raised so high they almost met his red hair. "Are they being punished for doing such a stupid thing?"

"Those two guards have lost their cushy jobs at the jail and are now riding in patrol cars looking for speeders. They've been at that job for only a few days, but already there's a stack of complaints from citizens who claim they've been unfairly treated. Beware of running into them! I hear they're issuing tickets to anything that moves."

Marie looked at her watch. "Time sure goes fast when you're having fun. Gotta go!" She jumped up from the table, kissed Tom on the head, patted Mitch on the shoulder, and disappeared through the door.

CHAPTER 31

"IT'S MY TURN TO DRIVE!" the officer protested as his partner beat him back to the patrol car. The partner was still brushing the powdered donut crumbs off his uniform as he slid under the wheel and turned the key.

"Sez who? Is it written somewhere that we have to take turns? Don't think so, buddy!"

"It's your fault that we're here to begin with," the loser pouted as he crawled into the passenger's seat and fastened his seat belt.

"What the hell do you mean by that? It's my fault? How do you figure that?"

"You were the one who decided it was fine to let the prisoner out of his cell."

"I didn't hear you objecting! You went right along with it. If you had said something, maybe I would have reconsidered. And, by the way," the driver smirked as he turned to his passenger, "I didn't know you *couldn't* sing."

"That's a terrible thing to say!"

"How can the truth be terrible? Didn't you see Ida giving you dirty looks? You were spoiling the good harmony she had going with the prisoner."

The passenger took a swipe at his eyes and slouched down in his seat. "This patrol duty is the pits. We really had it good back there in the jail."

"I don't know if this job is so bad. It's kinda fun issuing tickets. I like it when the women cry."

"You sure are a natural at it! Let's find someone and give them a ticket. I'm getting bored."

The two were driving on the road leading to Route 116, the road that would take them past the scenic lookout where the land dropped sharply down to the lake below. Since there was not much traffic, the lone pickup truck was easy to spot.

"Let's give the driver of that truck a ticket."

"What's he doing wrong?"

"Nothing, but we can make up something."

"Think that's a good idea? We're already in trouble. Don't forget all those complaints the captain was lecturing us about this morning."

"Serves him right for taking away our jail job!" The partner punched his fist into the air.

"That driver looks big. What if he puts up some kind of resistance? He really isn't doing anything wrong."

"You think he's gonna argue with two policemen? I don't think so. Put on the siren!"

Hearing the siren, Sammy, who was returning home from his shopping trip into town, raised his eyes and looked in his rear view mirror. He pulled to the side of the road, stopped, and rolled down the window. The two police officer got out of their patrol car and walked up to the open window.

"What seems to be the trouble, officers?"

"You were weaving across the white line. Please get out of the car."

Sammy was thinking fast as he opened the car door and stepped out. To his knowledge, he had done nothing wrong, but there was no way his identification as Frank Adams was going to stand up under scrutiny. He was not about to let his plans be spoiled by these two cops.

"Officers, I really don't believe I was driving erratically," he said quietly.

"Arguing with the law, are you? Turn around and put your hands on the truck!"

The driver pushed Sammy towards the truck while his partner grabbed his arm and twisted it. The knife that appeared in Sammy's other hand was so unexpected the partner never had a chance to make a sound. The driver turned in time to see his partner falling, but not soon enough to escape Sammy's knife. It was all over in seconds.

Sammy looked around. There was no traffic in sight. Here he was again at the scenic lookout, the one he had rolled Eileen Miller's body down after he had killed her, and the one he careened over after hitting the deer. He shook his head in disbelief as he pulled on a pair of old work gloves.

After moving the police car to the edge of the ravine, he struggled to get both bodies in without getting blood on his clothes. He shoved aside the dead cop in the front, shifted the gear to neutral, and then pushed. The car slowly started its journey down the steep hill, picking up speed as it went. When it came to rest in a thicket of newly budding spring underbrush, the car was scarcely visible from the road.

Sammy looked around. There were no witnesses. Scuffing his feet, he moved dirt onto the spilled blood on the road. Only his bloody gloves had visible evidence of a crime. Checking his clothes for stains and finding none, he crawled back into the old pickup and drove on.

CHAPTER 32

SARAH WAS FINISHING the lunch dishes when she heard the unmistakable sound of the old pickup coming down the driveway. Sammy was back and so was her feeling of dread. The morning without him had been so pleasant. To be honest, it had been more than pleasant. Working in the vineyard next to Albert had made her feel young, like a teenager. Their hands had touched by accident while tying up a young shoot. Albert's sudden intake of breath told her she wasn't the only one who had felt that sensation.

Shaking herself out of the daydream, she was back at the job of cleaning the kitchen when activity in the yard outside the window caught her eye. Sammy, who hadn't unloaded the supplies from the back of the truck, was standing by a pile of rubbish she had raked together last week in a feeble attempt at cleaning the yard. She watched with interest as he disappeared into the shed and came out with a can of gasoline. A few days ago, she had asked him to burn the pile so she wasn't surprised that he was going to do it. But why now? Since it hadn't rained in days and the leaves were dry, why did he need gasoline? He looked around, and seeing no one watching him, removed a balled-up something from his pocket. She watched him pour gasoline over the object and throw it on top of the pile. What in the world was he up to now? He was still holding the can when he lit the match.

Gas fumes from the can ignited and enveloped him in flames. Realizing she needed something to smother the flames, she stopped long enough to scoop up the large area rug by the kitchen table. By the time she got outside, he had not only succeeded in beating out the flames, he had managed to strike another match. Sarah watched the instant explosion of flames on the gasoline soaked object on top of the pile.

"What in the world is going on?" Sarah yelled. "You scared me half to death! Look at you!"

Sammy was cautiously taking inventory of his body. Other than the few seconds of sheer terror, there didn't seem to be any consequence from his little show. He wasn't experiencing any pain so he figured the flash fire hadn't burned him. What he really wanted to do was to check the pile of burning leaves to make sure the bloody gloves were gone; but, as usual, Smothering Sarah was right in his face.

"So what are you talkin' about?" Sammy asked in a harsh manner. "You know somethin' I don't?"

Sarah, seeing that he wasn't injured, burst into laughter. "I'm not saying another word until you go into the house and look at yourself in the mirror."

Giving her a dirty look, he picked up a stick with the pretext of stirring the fire. The gloves that were the only thing that would tie him to the murder of the two police officers were nothing but ashes. He grinned to himself as he headed for the house.

When you're good, you're good, and he certainly was.

CHAPTER 33

ALBERT SWIPED HIS DIRTY hand over his sweaty face. Digging holes was hard work and he hadn't done anything this strenuous in a long time. He groaned when he thought of the stiff muscles he was going to have in the morning. Looking around for his fellow workers, he was annoyed to find that he was the only one still digging. Sammy was in town picking up the rosebushes that would go into the holes, Sarah was at the house cleaning up after lunch, and Clarence was chasing a butterfly. "Hey Clarence!" he yelled as he stood and arched his back to soothe protesting muscles. "Pick up that shovel and get back to work!"

Looking chagrined, Clarence grabbed the shovel and started digging. Because his eyes were still following the brightly colored butterfly even as he shoveled, he was the first one to spot Sammy as he entered the vineyard. He dropped his shovel.

"Clarence, what are you up to now?" Albert scolded. "Leave that poor butterfly alone! Get to work!"

"But, but…" stammered Clarence.

"No buts about it! Sarah's gonna kick your lazy ass out if you don't pull your weight around here!"

"But, but Albert, look at Samm…Frank!" There was enough agitation in Clarence's voice to make Albert quit digging and look to where Clarence was pointing. Sammy was marching into the vineyard, head held high, daring anyone to laugh at his appearance. Albert, seeing how funny Sammy's face looked without eyebrows, burst into laughter. When he noticed that most of the beard and mustache were gone too, he sobered up. “What the hell happened to you?” he asked. “Playin’ with matches again?”

“Shut your damn mouth if you know what’s good for you! I seen myself in the mirror and it ain’t that bad.”

Albert smothered his chuckle. “I guess that’s a matter of opinion, buddy. You gonna tell us what you did?”

“None of your damn business! Now tell me how many holes you and Clarence dug while I was gone and,” he said as he poked Albert in the chest, “did you stay away from Sarah like I told you to? The answer to that last question had better be ‘yes’.”

Albert thought back to the morning when he and Sarah were working side by side tying up the baby shoots. The sun was warm on their backs as they tended the vines and he had experienced a peacefulness that he hadn’t felt in a long time. It was a feeling of contentment. It was a feeling that this place was where he was supposed to be and a feeling that, finally, he was home. That’s when their hands had touched.

Albert shook his head to chase away the morning memories. “Yes, I stayed away from Sarah. But if you’re plannin’ on courtin’ her in earnest, I really think you should wait until your eyebrows grow back,” he replied with unmistakable laughter in his voice.

“Watch your mouth! Looks like you have a lot more holes to dig, so get back to work,” he said as he turned to walk away.

“Hey, wait a damn minute! Where you goin? Think you’re too big to dig holes? We need a little help here!”

“Yeah,” agreed Clarence. “I’ve got blisters on top of blisters. How do you get out of diggin’?”

“I haven’t unloaded the truck yet. Quit pissin’! I’ll come back and dig after I’m done.” With that, he turned and walked back towards the house.

"Think we'll see him again today?" asked Clarence.

"Wouldn't bet on it." Albert was back shoveling.

"Albert, I'm not gonna tell," Clarence whispered.

"Tell what?" Albert stopped shoveling.

"I'm not gonna tell Sammy about you and Sarah. I seen what happened today."

"You seen what? There was nothing to see!" Albert held his breath. What had Clarence seen? All he needed now was more female problems. Sammy was just waiting for a chance to kick him out of Sarah's house.

"I'm not stupid, Albert. I saw the look on both your faces when your hands touched. But don't worry. I ain't talkin'."

Albert thought before he answered. "I admit that something is goin' on between Sarah and me. I didn't ask for it, and I'm not encouragin' it. I can't afford to, because Sammy will do somethin' bad to me. I'm a wanted man, but so is Sammy. I don't think he would tell the cops where I am, but he's not above getting' rid of me… permanently. I think you know what I mean."

Clarence nodded his head in agreement. "I know he intends to own this vineyard some day. Do you know how he plans on doin' that?"

"Before I showed up, his plan was to get Sarah to marry him and then get rid of her. Now that we're here, I think he has to change it."

Clarence's face clouded. "Get rid of Sarah? You mean k-k-kill her?"

"You surely know he's capable of doin' that! Why are you so surprised?"

"But I like Sarah! Albert, we can't let Sammy kill her!"

"Who's getting killed?" asked Sarah as she joined them.

Clarence and Albert jumped. They hadn't heard Sarah's quiet approach.

His heart was pounding, wondering how much of the conversation Sarah had heard. "We were talkin' about killin' weeds, weren't we, Clarence?" Albert finally managed to say.

"Yes, weeds! We was talkin' about killin' weeds!" Clarence forced a laugh.

"I must say you both were looking quite serious; the weeds should be scared to death! But really, I came out to see how many holes still need to be dug."

"Sarah," asked Albert, "do you know what happened to Frank?"

Sarah was suspicious of the burning incident, but she wasn't about to share her thoughts with these two. Obviously the three of them were connected in some way and, since she didn't know how, she was keeping her mouth shut. "I had asked Frank to get rid of pile of leaves that I had raked up last week. That's what he was doing today when he got burned."

"He got burned just trying to set fire to a pile of dry leaves? There has to be more to the story than that," a puzzled Albert reasoned.

"Uh, yes, there is more. For some reason he felt the pile needed some help to burn, so he got gasoline out of the shed and poured it on the pile."

"Talk about overkill!" laughed Albert. "So then what happened?"

"I saw him strike a match while he was still holding the gas can. All of a sudden, there was a flash, and Frank had flames all over him! Scared me to death!"

"But he didn't look burned!"

"That's right. Good thing the can was empty; it was just the fumes that ignited. He struck a second match and threw it on the pile of leaves, so at least the pile is gone."

"And so is the hair on his face!" quipped Clarence, and they all laughed.

Sarah's hungry eyes drank in the intoxicating sight of Albert's laughing face. When she removed the scarf from around her neck and tenderly wiped away the dirt on his forehead, it was Albert's face, not Larry's, that she touched.

This was the scene that Sammy witnessed when he returned to the vineyard.

CHAPTER 34

MOLLY WAS INTENT ON reading the morning paper. It had happened again. Two boys had disregarded the signs at the lookout on 116. Curiosity about the area where Sammy's car had been found was stronger than the warnings. Stumbling across the patrol car with the two dead police officers in it was a bit more than they had expected to find. Being typical teenagers, they had cell phones with them. A hysterical call to 911 brought an immediate response. According to the story she was reading, the boys were still being treated for shock.

Mitch walked into the breakfast area, poured himself a cup of coffee, and seated himself across from his wife. "Anything of interest?" he asked as he stirred the cream and sugar that he had loaded into his cup. "You're looking pensive, Molly. Something in the paper?"

Molly pushed the paper toward Mitch. "I was just remembering my grandparents in Pennsylvania. Grandpa Allen's favorite place to take strangers when they visit is called The Narrows. The road has been cut out of the hillside and the drop on the other side is so deep it takes your breath away. The view is similar to looking out of an airplane window. You can see the shape of the squared plowed fields and the farm houses look like toys."

"I take it this story is going somewhere?"

"Indulge me. This beautiful scenic spot is used by the locals as the town dump. Anything from refrigerators to old farm machinery and garbage is pushed over the top and it all rolls down the gorge and disappears."

"Interesting story. Is there an ending?"

"Read the headlines," Molly urged.

Picking up the paper, Mitch's eyes spotted the picture of a car being hauled out of the drop-off at the scenic lookout on Route 116. There was silence at the breakfast table while he read the story. He looked over the top of the paper at his wife. "I get your point. The scenic lookout is turning into our town's dump."

"It sure sounds like it. Think it could all be connected?"

"We know the first two things are," he replied. "Sammy got rid of Eileen's body by rolling her down that cliff. And as for as how his car got down there, when they examined it they found deer hairs embedded around the front lights. There probably was deer blood at one time, but the weather washed all that away. The theory is that Sammy hit a deer and went over the edge. But this last deal, a car with two dead policemen in it, doesn't seem to fit the mold."

"Mitch, you aren't putting the whole picture together! The escaped prisoner was part of Sammy's old gang, and those dead policemen were the same two who allowed the guy out of his cell."

"I didn't catch that, but you're right! Maybe we'll find that they do all tie in together. But I do know that in two days those cops had racked up more complaints from drivers who felt they had been unfairly ticketed than the department gets in an entire year."

"Maybe they just tried to give a ticket the wrong person," Molly mused.

"Don't you think murder would be a pretty drastic thing to do just to get out of paying a fine?" he asked.

"Depends on who they stopped. Say it was someone who didn't want his identification checked, or someone driving without a license, or maybe someone breaking parole, or some…."

"I get the picture, Molly. You make me wonder who the detective is in this family!"

Molly laughed. “No competition here, I promise. Just thinking.”

“Did you get any sleep last night? I heard you prowling around.”

Molly’s face clouded. “Not much. Dr. Parker hasn’t found the magic combination yet. But he’s trying. Mitch, how would you feel about my going back to work for a few hours a day? Clara needs a rest!”

“That’s fine with me. After all, Allen Real Estate belongs to you and you’ve been out of the office a long time now, but do you think Anita is up to taking care of the twins?”

“As long as we do the night duty and allow her to sleep, I’m sure she can,” Molly reasoned.

Mitch yawned. “I’m walking around all day like a zombie. I ran into your brother and Marie at the hospital cafeteria and she couldn’t resist telling me how bad I looked. She wanted to know if you looked just as bad.”

“I haven’t looked in a mirror lately, and now I don’t think I ever will! At least not until the twins sleep through the night.”

“Does that ever happen?” Mitch rubbed his eyes.

“I hear that teenagers sleep a lot. Can you wait that long?” Molly asked as she refilled their coffee mugs.

Mitch groaned, pushed the breakfast dishes out of the way, and laid his head on the table.

CHAPTER 35

MOLLY UNLOCKED THE DOOR to her office and stepped inside. Clara hadn't arrived yet and the dark office seemed strange and unfamiliar to her. This had been her sole terrain for years. It was an eerie feeling to have the sense that someone else lived here now. It even smelled different. Her eyes were drawn to the dark stain on the floor. That's where Sammy had stood bleeding from the bullet wound in his shoulder. It still made her smile when she recalled the horrified look on his face when her water had broken and splashed on his foot. He had run out of the office and disappeared. His car had been found, but Sammy was still missing.

She shook her head to remove any remaining anxious thoughts and reached for the light switch. Clara had taken possession of her office and had even rearranged the file cabinets. She had every right to make those changes, and Molly decided she wouldn't even mention it.

Clara had done an amazing number of transactions while Molly was gone. Even after giving Clara a bigger percent of the commissions, rewarding the two mothers for their help, and paying Joe the fireman for putting the signs in front yards, Allen Real Estate was in the black. It had never before boasted such a healthy, robust bank account.

She was deep in thought when the door burst open and two laughing people and a huge dog rushed in. Seeing Molly, the people stopped abruptly, but not the dog. Lucky knew a friend when he smelled one, and he raced across the room and came to a skidding stop at her feet. "Now I know what it must feel like to be almost hit by an eighteen-wheeler!" Molly laughed, "And I see Lucky hasn't made any headway in the manners department either!" She used the sleeve of her jacket to wipe her face that was now devoid of make-up.

A flustered Clara and an amused Joe were still standing by the open office door. "Molly! What a surprise! I didn't know you were coming to the office today!" Clara was clearly apprehensive. In Molly's absence, she had usurped her office; all traces of the former occupant were gone. Had she even a thought that Molly was planning on showing up today she would have retrieved her things from the closet.

"Good morning to you, too," Molly grinned as she pushed Lucky away. "Your dog sure seems happy that I'm back!"

"Lucky has his favorites, and you have always been one of them. But Molly, are you just here to visit?"

"Sort of, but I think it's about time I got back to work. Clara, I can't believe what you have accomplished while I was away having the twins! I was going over the books last night and the number of transactions you have handled is staggering. It made me feel so guilty that I wasn't here to help you," Molly said as she crossed the room and hugged Clara. "My goodness!" she exclaimed as she stepped back. "There's not much left of you to hug!"

Clara laughed. "Remember all those diets I went on?"

Molly screwed up her face and held her nose. "The one I remember the best was the egg diet. It didn't work any better than the rest, but for some reason it's the one that sticks in my memory."

Joe had been quietly watching the reunion of the two women. Clara, who had started out as Molly's secretary, was now a successful realtor. The love he felt for Clara as he watched her animated face had been slow in coming, but it had come. He had no idea how Clara felt about him. Other than putting the signs in front yards for her, their sole contact with each other revolved around Lucky. Even stopping for lunch on the daily walk was out of the question because no restaurant wanted a dog that looked like a bear tied up outside its door.

Molly smiled as she watched Joe's face and wondered if Clara had any idea how smitten he was with her. "Are you still getting new business?" she asked. "Lucky hasn't done anything outrageous in a long time."

"You want him to do something more outrageous than what he did at Christmas?" Clara looked incredulous. "Is there anything more extreme than attacking Santa?"

After the merriment had died down, Clara asked, "Molly, do you remember when you said you didn't have to advertise your services because of repeat and referral business?"

Molly nodded her head. "I do. But you haven't been in the business long enough for repeat customers."

"Something you said stuck in my memory," Clara said, "and I didn't forget it no matter how unreasonable the buyer or seller became."

Molly had an amused look on her face. "I said something profound? I can't wait to hear what it was!"

"You said, 'A satisfied customer is worth his weight in gold.' Almost all my new business now comes from referrals from satisfied customers."

"That's how it works! I have many satisfied customers, so does anyone ever call and ask for me? Or have I been away so long no one remembers me?" There was a sad note in Molly's voice.

"You haven't been away that long, Girlfriend! Many people call and ask for you, and some weren't too happy to find that they had to work with me. So it's time for you to come back!"

"I plan to, but just on a part-time basis. Anita is good, but until the twins settle down into a regular routine, I need to be around to help her. Not to change the subject, but what is Lucky doing?" Molly asked as she pointed at the dog.

"He sniffing," Clara said. "I call that stain 'Sammy's calling card'."

"That's interesting," Molly said with a thoughtful look on her face. "Do you know anything about tracking dogs? I wonder if one of those dogs can match up old blood's smell with the person the blood came from? Since Lucky seems to be the 'result of many generations of doggy backyard sex', to quote you, there probably is a bit of bloodhound in him along with everything else."

"What an idea!" Clara was laughing. "The next outrageous thing Lucky can do to bring more business our way is to track down the missing Sammy! I can see the headlines in the morning paper already!"

Joe, who had been silent, finally joined the conversation. "You really think Sammy is just going to come to town and walk down the street? I don't think so. Too many people know what he looks like." He glanced over at Clara who had the grace to blush.

Molly was having fun with the idea. "You have to admit it would be a great ending to the Sammy saga if Lucky tracked him down because of the smell of that bloodstain."

"That's pretty far-fetched! Come to think of it, it was the smell of his cologne that tripped him up the first time. But Joe's right. Sammy would have to be walking around town for Lucky even to get a chance to smell him and I don't believe that's going to happen. And we wouldn't need a dog to sniff him out!"

"What if he's changed his appearance?" Joe asked quietly.

Clara snorted. "To make that happen, he'd have to lose his brilliant smile, his blond crew-cut, and his six pack abs. I don't think so."

Joe shrugged. "Just a thought!" he said. "Come on, Lucky, let's go."

Lucky took one last sniff of Sammy's calling card and followed Joe out the door.

CHAPTER 36

SAMMY STORMED INTO THE vineyard, his distorted face looking as menacing as his raised shovel. Sarah, puzzled by his obvious fury, backed away from Albert.

"What the hell do you think you're doin'?" he shouted at Albert.

Sarah studied Albert, curious to see what he was doing that had made Sammy so angry. Since he was just standing there, Sarah yelled. "Put down that shovel! Albert's not doing anything!"

"The hell he ain't!" Sammy bellowed. "Sarah, go to the house, now!"

"I will not!" She crossed her arms and stomped her foot. "Who are you to order me around? This is my vineyard, and don't you forget it!"

"Sarah," said Albert quietly, "Go."

Alarmed, she looked at both of them. Frank was brandishing the shovel, but Albert, although his face was white, hadn't moved. "Sorry, Albert, but I'm not leaving until Frank quits acting like an idiot! Put down that shovel, Frank! This is ridiculous! I was standing right by Albert so I know he wasn't doing anything!"

"Ha! That's where you're wrong, missy! Now go along like a good little girl and let us men settle our differences," he said dismissively as he gave Sarah a hard shove towards the house.

"Take your hands off her!" Albert shouted as he lunged for Sammy, his fists raised. Jumping aside to deflect Albert's punch, Sammy lost his balance. When the shovel slipped out of his hand and landed at Sarah's feet, she snatched it off the ground. Holding it close to her body, she ran. Clarence, who had backed away from the group the moment he had seen Sammy approaching, ran after her.

"Clarence," Sammy roared, "you get your butt back here!"

Reluctantly, Clarence stopped, turned around, and slowly walked back to the vineyard. He hated violence, but he was sure that violence was what he was about to witness.

Desperate to find out what was going on, Sarah hid behind a big oak tree at the edge of the vineyard. Although she was too far away to hear, she wasn't too far away to see what was going on. Clarence had been running behind her, but now she saw that he had turned back and was joining the other two. *Thick as thieves.* Those were the words that were running through her head as she watched the three of them. *Thick as thieves.* She had to keep thinking of that evil man as *Frank.* Just one slip and Sammy would know she was on to him. Her life depended on not making that one slip.

Sammy, shouting, moved so close to Albert she was sure he was spraying spit on Albert's face. When Albert pulled back his arm, fist clenched, prepared to take a swing, she covered her eyes with her hands. Peeking around her fingers, she relaxed when she saw Clarence rush to stand between the two men. Sammy was still pointing his finger and yelling when Albert abruptly turned and walked off. Sarah slipped from behind the tree and ran for the house.

Back in the vineyard, Sammy was trying to rein in his rage. "Do you think Albert got the message?" he asked.

Clarence was shaking. "I should hope so! I know I did." He turned to look at Sammy as he emphasized the next word, "Frank."

"That's right! My name is Frank, and you better not forget it! You two have been callin' me Sammy when we're together, but you gotta cut it out! I don't know what Sarah heard that day in town when my car was found, but she might put two and two together."

Clarence looked worried. “Why would you think she didn’t hear anythin’? Women talk.”

“I’ve had my suspicions. But I ain’t seen any difference in her behavior towards me since that day.”

“What if she’s pretendin’?”

Sammy snorted. “She ain’t no actress! I’d spot it in a minute.”

“You said they was still talkin’ about you the last time you went into town.”

“Yes, they were,” he grinned. “It was like playin’ hide and seek, only I wasn’t hidin’. I was walkin’ right besides them, listenin’ to them talkin’ about me!”

“Sarah mentioned her new hair-do needed a trim. That means a trip back to the beauty shop.”

Sammy thought. “Guess we can’t let her do that.”

“How you gonna stop her?”

“You let me worry about that.”

Clarence was quiet. “Samm….Frank, did you mean what you said?”

“I always mean what I say, and don’t you forget it!”

“Did you mean it when you said you’d have to kill her?”

“Do I have a choice? Or maybe I should say, do *we* have a choice?”

“What *we* are you talkin’ about?”

“Do you have a short memory, or are you just plain stupid, Clarence?”

“Samm…Frank, there you go again, makin’ me feel bad!”

“Well, think for a change! All three of us are wanted men. You and Albert broke into a house, so you’re not lily white. Albert maybe killed a lady when he escaped from jail and the police have been looking for me since last November.”

Clarence, his face contorted, cried, “I like livin’ here on the vineyard, and I really don’t want Sarah to find out who we are. But I don’t understand what you’re up to! If you’re gonna kill Sarah anyway, why do you care if Albert is payin' attention to her? You and that shovel was pretty scary!"

"Albert won't be payin' any more attention to Miss Sarah; I have plans. And as for Sarah, I will be lookin' for any hint that she knows who I am."

Clarence hung his head. "And then you'll kill her?"

Sammy whirled and grabbed Clarence's shirt collar with both hands. "I know you're soft on her because I see how you look at her. But if you think I'm not capable of doing away with Miss Sarah and *any of her close friends*, you'd better think again!"

Clarence regained his balance. "I sure hope that doesn't have to happen," he said fervently. "And what you threatened to do to Albert if he don't leave Sarah alone was pretty scary too. Albert really didn't do nothin'! Sarah was just wipin' some dirt off his face. I don't know what you thought was goin' on when you came into the vineyard wavin' that shovel!"

"Don't give me that drivel! Albert knew exactly what he was doin', Clarence."

"Doin' what? He was just standin' there doing nothin' when Sarah wiped his face! What did he do that was so terrible?"

"Clarence, I have a plan. Some day this vineyard is gonna be mine. I just haven't figured out how it's gonna happen, but at the beginning I was hopin' to get it through Sarah. Now if she gets sweet on Albert because he looks like her dead husband, that's gonna put a wrench in that plan. If I have to do away with Albert to prevent this from happenin', that's what I'm gonna do!"

"Albert didn't look too good when you told him that. He was pretty shook up."

"He's gonna be more than shook up when I'm done with him. Let's head back to the house and see what Sarah's made for dinner."

"I don't know how you can be so unfeelin," Clarence was struggling to keep up with Sammy's long legs. "You're talkin' about killin' and hurtin' people like it was the most natural thing for you to do."

"Clarence, for me it is the natural thing to do. I've survived this long because I have a very strong sense of self-preservation and I'm not stoppin' now."

Albert was nowhere to be seen when it came time for dinner. Sarah didn't ask any questions as she removed his place setting from the table. The simple meal of soup and sandwiches was eaten in silence.

The charged atmosphere in the house was almost palpable; Albert's absence was not mentioned. There was no laughter around the card table.

Bedtime came early as the three made excuses and retreated to their rooms.

CHAPTER 37

SAMMY GLANCED AT HIMSELF in the rear view mirror as he pulled onto the main road, heading into town. He had tried to downplay the damage the flash fire had done to his appearance, but the mirror told it all. Big sunglasses did a good job of hiding the fact that his eyebrows were missing.

He could tell Sarah was smothering her amusement when she had trimmed the remaining hair on his face. When her scissors slipped and nicked his cheek, the fright on her face at the sight of his blood pleased him. Although it had been just a surface cut, it hadn't stopped bleeding. He blotted the bleeding cut with a tissue and stuck it into his pocket.

Concerned that his changed appearance would draw attention, he wouldn't have taken the chance of being recognized if the trip into town hadn't been necessary. Albert had made it necessary.

The unsettling scene in the vineyard had been a wake-up call. He hoped the warning he had given Albert was scary enough to calm down any amorous feelings he might be harboring for Sarah. The problem, he had to admit, was with Sarah. Her reaction to Albert was something he couldn't do a thing about. But he could do something about Albert, and so the trip to town.

Turning off the ignition, he glanced at his image in the mirror one more time. He grimaced at the reflection. The face and body he had before the accident was only a memory now. One thing was the same.

He smiled with satisfaction as he took a deep breath and inhaled the heady scent of his cologne.

There were several ways to get rid of Albert, or Sarah if he needed to, and this trip into town was to stockpile the necessary items for one or the other. He figured he could buy the lye without too many questions being asked. It was common practice to cover the carcasses of road and coyote kill with lye to hold down the odor. He also needed a body bag to hold the lye-covered body while it dissolved. Making up believable stories had always been easy for him, but buying a body bag would need a better story than even he could dream up.

He was so deep in thought as he walked down the street that at first he didn't notice the clicking of claws on the sidewalk. When he did become aware of the sound, he turned and almost yelled aloud. Miss Piggy's black dog stood behind him, sniffing. He had seen this dog before. The first time was when he had stumbled onto a dogfight and ended up poking this very same dog bloody with a sharp stick; the second time was at that fateful Sunday open house. In fact, the dog had pulled off his shoe when he jumped out the window and landed on the cop. "Go away, dog," he said in a stern voice, and continued his walk. When the clicking noise behind him started again, he turned and shouted, "I said git!"

The dog just looked into Sammy's eyes and sniffed.

From across the street a man ran out of Allen Real Estate and yelled, "Lucky! Where are you?" Seeing the dog, the man disregarded traffic and sprinted across the street to grab Lucky's collar.

Not wanting to talk to anyone, Sammy said quietly, "No harm done," and tried to walk away.

Lucky was not giving up. He was trying to stick his nose into the man's pocket when Joe pulled roughly on his collar and dragged him back to the office. Clara, who had been on the phone, asked, "What was all that about?"

"You got me!" Joe answered. "Have you ever seen Lucky do anything like that before?"

"Do what? I was on the phone."

"He must have gotten out the door when your last buyer left the office. When I finally saw him across the street, he was sniffing that guy that I had seen once before in town. Remember those two characters who crashed their bikes outside our office? They wanted to know if there were any new people in town and that guy was the only one I could think of."

"Did you ever find out who he is?"

"No. This is only the second time I've seen him."

"Wonder why Lucky was so attracted to him."

Joe laughed. "He smelled good! Lucky was probably hoping the smell was coming from something he could eat."

"Maybe he's practicing," Clara chuckled.

"Practicing for what?"

"Remember when we said we needed Lucky to do another outrageous thing to bring in more business? Maybe Lucky was listening to us. Think so?"

"Lucky's special, but not that special," observed Joe.

Lucky, who was curled up in the corner half asleep, raised his head and snorted.

"I don't think Lucky agrees with your opinion," snickered Clara. "How does it feel to be dismissed by a dog?"

"Compared to Brenda, Lucky's an amateur. I didn't feel a thing!" Joe said as he bent down and scratched Lucky's ears. "I apologize for saying you aren't special because you are. Forgive me?"

Lucky, happy to have his ears scratched, gave Joe a sloppy kiss.

"Ugh!" sputtered Joe.

"Way to go, Lucky!" hooted Clara.

Lucky used his nose to push his empty dish towards Clara.

CHAPTER 38

THINGS HAD CHANGED. There was an undercurrent Sarah felt but didn't understand. Whatever happened, it had changed the way Albert looked at her; in fact, he avoided looking at her. When he left the room that she entered, the intensity of her disappointment and hurt surprised her. He no longer ate his meals with them, nor did he join them in the evening activities. In the morning, empty containers in the sink were the only evidence that he was eating. At first, she thought it strange that neither Clarence nor Sammy commented on Albert's behavior, because they acted as if nothing had changed. That was when she realized that she was the only one who didn't know what was going on. This was not a good feeling.

Clarence was another mystery. Sarah caught him looking at her with eyes full of concern. They reminded her of her mom's eyes when Sarah had left home for college. And when Albert and Sammy were working in the same area of the vineyard, he managed to position himself between them.

Since today's rain kept them from the vineyard, she'd made a hair appointment with Betty. Sarah loved her short hair. However, there was a problem with short hair; it grew. For some reason, Clarence seemed uneasy when he offered to do the lunch dishes so she could spruce herself up a bit for the trip into town.

The eyes of all three men were on her as she descended the staircase. It made her feel like a princess and she flaunted herself a bit.

"Wow," said Clarence, placing the dishtowel over his shoulder, "You sure do look nice!"

Albert smiled, opened his mouth to say something, but changed his mind when Clarence nudged him. It was then she noticed that Sammy's eyes were not on her; they were staring hard at Albert. What was going on?

"Does anyone need anything from town? I'll be glad to pick it up for you if you do." Sarah was so anxious to get out of this house she practically babbled. She looked at each man separately. No one was moving. Clarence still had the concerned look in his eye, Albert wouldn't look directly at her, and Sammy had a smirk on his face.

"Well, if nothing is needed, I'll be on my way," she said as she breezed past the three and headed for the hook by the door where the truck keys always hung. There were no keys.

"One of you has the keys in his pocket?" she asked hopefully. Silence. She turned around and faced them. "Come on, hand them over! I have an appointment!" Clarence's eyes were on the floor, Albert's face was red, and Sammy was still smirking. Her initial anger was fast changing into panic. The impact of the situation hit her like a brick. She had foolishly let herself believe she could co-exist with these men if she just kept her eyes and mouth shut. However, whatever happened that day in the vineyard had led to this.

She smiled a shaky smile and tried to keep her voice from quivering. "Frank, I think you were the last one to use the truck. Did you misplace the keys? Should we help you look for them?"

Sammy pulled his hand out of his pocket and dangled the keys. "The keys ain't lost."

Sarah held out her hand and she was surprised that it was relatively steady. "Could I have them, please?"

Sammy gave her the smirk again and slid the keys back into his pocket. "I don't think so, missy. I suggest you forget about your trip to town."

"Forget about my appointment? For what reason? We can't work in the fields today because it's too wet." She tried to keep her voice steady.

"All three of us feel it's in our best interest that you don't go into town."

"All three of you?" She tried to look at Albert but he turned his face away; Clarence was still looking at the floor. "What kind of talk is that? I don't understand!"

"There are some things that it's best you don't understand. That's why you ain't goin' into town."

"Just today? If I can't go today, when can I go?" Her legs were about to fail her.

"That's for us to decide, not you." Sammy's smile was pure evil.

She thought fast and put up a bold front. "This is my vineyard and don't you three forget it! But if you say I can't go into town today, I need to call the shop and cancel my appointment."

Of course, the number she intended to call was 911. The three watched her march haughtily across the room and pick up the phone.

There was no dial tone.

CLARA SHOOK THE WATER off her dripping umbrella and stepped into the lively atmosphere of the beauty shop. Every station was filled. Being squeezed into Betty's busy schedule didn't look too promising for a drop-in appointment.

Betty, hearing the bell over the door ring as it opened, looked up and saw Clara standing at the front desk. "I know you don't have an appointment, Clara, so are you just looking for a dry place to grab a free cup of coffee?" she joked.

"Even free, your coffee isn't worth getting wet for," Clara fired back.

The women in the shop laughed at the exchange. The beauty shop was living up to its lively reputation.

"So what can I do for you?" Betty asked as she continued to cut an elderly lady's purple hair.

"Molly's working for a few hours today, so I thought it would be a good time to slip out and get my hair trimmed. I know I don't have an appointment, and it looks like I'm out of luck."

"Not so fast, Clara! I think I have an opening. It looks like my two o'clock is a no-show."

"Really?" Clara raised her eyebrows. "That doesn't happen to you very often, does it?"

"No, it doesn't, and I'm really surprised in this case. The woman was so glad when I told her I had an opening this afternoon she thanked me several times. She said she was looking forward to the appointment because it had been so exciting the day she was here. Seems she feels isolated out there on the peninsula."

"Where on the peninsula?" asked Clara, settling down with a six-month-old magazine that had seen better days, "and what happened that was so exciting?"

"Almost at the end of the peninsula, I think she said. She's been here only one time. It was the day the man escaped from jail and Sammy's car was found."

"Arc you sure?"

"Come to think of it, she got agitated when you popped your head in and yelled that Sammy's car had been found. She couldn't wait for me to finish telling her how to take care of her new cut. She threw two twenties on the counter and ran out. I was going to give her some change back today because no way did her haircut cost forty dollars, but it looks like she's not coming."

A woman getting a manicure chimed in. "I was in here that day, too, and I recognized the woman you're talking about. She's a widow, has been for over a year now."

Betty looked thoughtful. "From what she told me, she owns a vineyard. I thought she had a husband because she talked about working the vines with someone. Must have hired a worker."

Betty's purple-haired customer was listening to the conversation. "I live near that woman but I don't know much about her. I do know that the vineyard was previously owned by a man named Paul Blakeman who died quite suddenly. That woman and her husband inherited the place, but then the husband died as suddenly as Paul. Must be a family trait!"

"Is she running that vineyard all by herself?" asked Clara. "I don't see how that's possible."

"I didn't see anyone else around the vineyard for a long time," the woman continued, "then in late November, I noticed that a man was living there too. Maybe a worker, because I see him driving by in that old pick-up truck of hers."

"What does he look like?" Clara asked. She was thinking of the stranger that Lucky had selected to sniff yesterday.

"Pretty scruffy, if you ask me!" snorted the purple-haired woman. "Long gray hair, looks like a bird's nest, and broken front teeth. I'm surprised she allows him to hang around, but she's probably hard up for workers."

Betty put down her scissors and went to the reception desk. "I don't have a good feeling about this," she said as she picked up the phone and dialed Sarah's number.

CHAPTER 39

SARAH FLIPPED HER pillow over, hoping to find a spot that wasn't wet. Judging by the light coming through the window she figured the time to be late afternoon. It seemed to her that she had been locked in her bedroom forever, but it wasn't even dinnertime. There were no cooking smells coming up from the kitchen either. Earlier today Sammy had said he was putting a surprise in the slow cooker for tonight's dinner. Maybe the big surprise was that there wasn't going to be a dinner, at least not for her. How long could they keep her locked up? Sammy said all three of them had decided that it was not in their best interest for her to go to town. Were the other two as dangerous as Sammy?

She hadn't had a chance against the three men. What had made her think she could live in the midst of the likes of them and not have it end badly? Something puzzled her. Albert's face, when Sammy had picked her up and thrown her over his shoulder, was ashen. When he winked at her and shook his head so minimally, she almost questioned what she was seeing. What was all that about? Was he sending her a message, or was it just his way of telling her he was sorry about what was happening?

After Sammy had dumped her onto the bed and they clomped out of her room, the sound of the key turning in the lock intensified her growing fear. What if Sammy had found out that she already knew who he was? She shuddered.

Hoping to learn their next move, she had stretched out on the floor with her ear near the register. They were talking in hushed voices, but every so often the conversation got loud and a few words came through. There wasn't a comforting word among them. Then it got quiet, and she hadn't heard a sound from downstairs in hours.

Exhausted from crying, she finally fell into a troubled sleep.

CLARENCE AND ALBERT confronted Sammy at the bottom of the stairs after the unceremonious dumping of Sarah. "Why the hell are we doin' this?" Albert was steaming. "Aren't we in enough trouble already? I don't even want to think about what the punishment is for holdin' someone prisoner in their own home!"

"Hold your water, Albert, and who do you think you are, actin' so high and mighty? Your nose ain't any cleaner than mine. You want her goin' into town and yakkin' with all those biddies in the beauty shop? It's a small town, and everyone in it knows that my car was found and that the escaped prisoner killed a nice lady on his way out."

"I don't think I killed her," Albert said defensively.

"Oh yes you did! Remember I went into town to hear what people on the street were talkin' about? She's dead, Albert," Sammy lied, "so you're no better than I am, and don't you forget it!"

Albert's face clouded and he hung his head. He'd say a prayer for the Church Lady if only he could remember how to pray. He was brought back to the unpleasant present when Clarence yelled and stamped his foot, "I didn't kill no one and I didn't escape from no jail, so don't count me in this holdin' Sarah prisoner thing! I don't like it one bit!"

"Don't pull that innocent thing on me, Clarence. Albert told me all about you breakin' into that house and don't forget the microwave you blew up. That's hangin' over your head, buddy."

It was a subdued lot that gathered in the kitchen. Clarence was holding back tears. He knew what they were doing to Sarah was wrong, but his fear of Sammy was keeping him quiet. Looking for an ally, he searched Albert's face hoping to see some sign of remorse. To his surprise, Albert winked. He was trying to figure out the wink when Albert broke the silence.

"Is there anything we should be doin' in the vineyard?"

"If there is, the only one who knows is Sarah, and I'm not about to go upstairs and ask her. Either of you want to volunteer?" Sammy sneered. No one volunteered.

In the vineyard, the weeds were growing and the insects were eating. Three of the rosebushes looked like they were on their last legs and, if the men had a radio to turn on, they would have learned that a freeze was predicted for the peninsula tonight.

CHAPTER 40

"HE'S DOING WHAT?" Clara held the phone away from her ear and eyed it suspiciously. "I don't think I heard you right, so tell me again."

"Lucky won't go inside now, even at night." Joe's voice was somewhere between laughter and exasperation.

"That's weird, even for Lucky!"

"Beyond weird," Joe agreed. "He paces back and forth, looking up one side of the street and then down the other."

"You think he's looking for something?"

"Or someone." Joe shrugged. "Your guess is as good as mine."

"When did this strange behavior start, Joe?" Clara was concerned. This was her dog they were talking about.

Joe was quiet while he thought. "I do believe it started the day he ran away."

"The day you found him sniffing the guy that smelled good?"

"That's the day!" Joe replied in a positive voice.

"You never told me what you smelled. I just figured it was some kind of food that lured Lucky across the street."

"It definitely wasn't food. It was some kind of cologne. One of the local stores has a fancy bottle of the stuff displayed in their window. Out of curiosity, I went in the other day and took a whiff. From the price of it I'm surprised they didn't charge me to smell it."

Clara was silent. "Did you get a really good look at the guy?"

"Well, yes. I already described to you what he looked like."

"His eyes. You didn't describe his eyes. Did you see his eyes?" Clara sat up straighter.

"No, the big sunglasses covered a lot of his face, and what the glasses didn't cover, the hair on his face did," Joe added slowly, wondering what Clara was thinking.

"Tell me about his teeth," she demanded, talking fast.

Joe heard the change in her voice. "Where are you going with this, Clara? I told you he had no upper teeth that I could see, well, I think I saw some broken-off front ones. In fact, he kept running his tongue over them."

"What did he say to you when you pulled Lucky away from him?"

"It was obvious he didn't want to talk to me. He just said something like 'no harm done' and walked away. What's this all about?"

Blushing, Clara laughed, and the edge went out of her voice. "Did I ever tell you that my girlhood hero was Nancy Drew? I spent my childhood looking for clues that would solve mysteries that happened only in my imagination."

"Sounds like something you never outgrew," Joe laughed. "So tell me, in your imagination, who is that mystery man?"

"Sammy." Clara said the name so quietly Joe wasn't quite sure he had heard correctly.

"Sammy? You think that man is Sammy?" Joe's voice raised in disbelief. "You think the guy the whole country has been looking for would just walk through town?"

"Remember the question you asked the other day? You said, 'What if he changed his appearance?'" Clara was talking fast.

"Yes, I remember. So what?"

"A dog wouldn't notice the change of appearance in a person because it wouldn't matter; the person would still smell the same." Clara paused, not quite sure how Joe was going to react. "I'm saying Lucky is on to something."

Joe didn't reply immediately. He had the feeling Clara was holding her breath. He spoke slowly. "I don't know if your suspicion has any merit, but I don't think I want to be around when you try to sell your Nancy Drew theory to the police."

The silence on the other end of the phone spoke volumes; Joe got the message because Brenda had taught him well. Back-peddling fast, he changed his tactics. "Uh, maybe we can find where that guy hangs out when he's not in town. I've seen him twice now."

Clara gasped and hit her forehead with the palm of her hand. "Listen to this, Joe! I just remembered! Why didn't I think of this before? The other day in the beauty shop a woman who lives out on the peninsula was talking about Betty's no-show. Betty was surprised when her two o'clock appointment didn't show up because she had been so happy that Betty could work her into her afternoon schedule. According to the woman, the no-show is a widow who owns a vineyard and has a scruffy handyman. Now, get this Joe! The first time the woman noticed that the widow wasn't living alone was last November. Last November, Joe! That's when Sammy went over the cliff! That's what happened to his brilliant smile! His teeth got knocked out!"

"Calm down, Clara," Joe urged.

"Calm down?" she yelled. "Why should I calm down? Lucky is trying to tell us he found the source of the smell on the office floor!"

"You think that's who he's looking for?" Joe couldn't believe he was going along with her theory. "He's afraid if he goes inside the station he'll miss Sammy the next time he comes to town?"

"Who knows how that dog thinks, Joe? I sure don't! Who do you think I should run this by?"

"Wait a minute! You're asking me to pick who I think would even listen to this wild theory of yours?"

"Yes I am! Now, think this through with me. Tom was stabbed by Sammy, so I think he would listen, but then Mitch is pretty anxious to get his hands on him because of the way he treated Molly right here in this office. So which one do I call?"

Knowing he was not going to talk her out of anything, he gave in. "Why don't you call both of them to your office and tell them?" Then for good measure, he added, "I'd like to be there too."

Clara released the breath she was holding. "Thanks for going along with me, Joe. I hope Tom and Mitch are as willing to listen to me as you were."

After ending the call to Joe, Clara sat in the quiet office for several minutes before she picked up the phone and dialed Tom's cell phone.

CHAPTER 41

THE SOUND OF HAIL hitting the window jarred Sarah from a troubled sleep. The only point of light in the dark room was the luminous face of the clock. Exhausted from terror and tears, she was amazed that she had been able to intermittently sleep the day away and part of the night. When she realized the sound she was hearing was hail, she jumped out of bed. Her vines! What were the men doing to protect her vines? Did any one of them even know how to do it? In her haste to turn on the light, she bumped into something. The splash of liquid on her leg and the clatter of silverware as it hit the floor prepared her for what she saw when she managed to get to the light switch. What had been her dinner lay in a cold lump on the rug by her bed. Someone had come into her room and left her food. She shuddered at the thought that one of the men had stood by her bed and watched her as she slept.

The hail stopped abruptly. Since there was no sound of activity in the house, she prayed they were all at the vineyard trying to figure out how to save the vines from the frost. Hoping to see lights and activity, she ran to the window. Her heart sank when all she saw was darkness.

Tears filled her eyes and once again she apologized to Larry. Her loneliness and stupidity had led to this. She was locked in a room when she should be burning smudge pots to keep the frost from settling on the vines. But then, maybe they weren't her vines any more. That thought brought more tears.

Now that things had come to this, could the men ever free her? Alarmed by that thought, she threw herself on the bed and sobbed in frustration. How long did they think they could keep her a prisoner in her own home? Maybe they wouldn't bother to keep her a prisoner. Maybe they intended to kill her.

Stark reality of the danger she was in propelled her off the bed and to the window. The ground below looked a mile away. Maybe if she tied sheets together...she shook her head. That only worked in movies.

Discouraged, she wandered into the closet. She had been in there hundreds of times so she had no hope that there was anything in it that could possibly help her, but it was the one place left that still had Larry's comforting smell. In the middle of all his work clothes, there hung the suit, the one he had worn on their wedding day. She buried her face in the soft material and breathed in the essence that had once been Larry. Since she hadn't had the heart to remove his clothes, his side of the closet looked as if he were still sharing the bedroom with her. She sighed. If she lived through this nightmare, getting rid of Larry's things would be an unpleasant but necessary thing she had to do.

Looking down, she saw the unrolled sleeping bag that had filled one whole corner of his side for over a year. She smiled, remembering the fun they'd had on their last camping trip that had ended when a monstrous rainstorm leveled their tent. When both soggy bags had finally dried, she had rolled hers up into a tidy bundle, but Larry had dropped dead before he gotten around to doing his. After his funeral, she had never been able to make herself finish the job. Now with nothing else to do, she pulled it out and started rolling.

Something caught her eye on the wall in the back of the newly empty corner. She sighed again and tried not to feel too guilty about her failing to keep her house clean; there just weren't enough hours in the day. Thinking she was going to find nothing but dust bunnies to brush off the wall, she was surprised to uncover a round object. She pushed Larry's clothes aside to give her more room; the round thing was some sort of knob. How had she not seen this before? Had Larry ever noticed it? Holding her breath, she twisted the knob and pulled. A door about four feet tall and four feet wide reluctantly opened. It was dark in the closet, but even in the dim light, she could see she was looking at a storage area.

Running back to her nightstand to retrieve her emergency flashlight, her bare foot stepped on something mushy. Startled, she covered her mouth. If what she had just stepped on was a spider, she knew she was going to scream. She hated spiders! With dread, she lifted her foot. When she saw that it was mashed potatoes and not a smashed spider that oozed between her toes, she felt almost faint with relief. Her forgotten dinner was still on the floor, just another thing to be cleaned up…later. However, the sight of food reminded her of how hungry she was and her stomach growled. Yesterday's lunch was a dim memory that had been so overshadowed by the events that followed, it seemed a lifetime ago.

Outside, dawn was threatening to break the hold of night on the land. Would she smell breakfast being cooked? Would someone remember to bring her something to eat? Her stomach growled again.

Back in the closet, now armed with a flashlight, she pointed the beam directly into the storage area. The space was full of boxes, lots and lots of dust-covered boxes. There was nothing written on the outside of any of them, nor were they sealed. Some had more dust on the top, indicating that the boxes had been stored at different times.

Picking one at random, she sat down on the floor, wiped the dust off the top of the box with her sleeve, and opened it. The object on top was a Raggedy Ann doll, which either had been loved to death, or had disintegrated with passing time. She pulled out art work that had decorated the front of someone's refrigerator, a bag of colorful marbles, a stack of report cards, some with a primly handwritten note stating the 'student hadn't lived up to her potential', and finally at the bottom of the box, written in Old English script, was a diploma. It was proof that, in spite of not 'living up to her potential' Beth Ann Williams had managed to graduate from high school. Had Beth Ann been the wife of Uncle Paul? The only time she had met Uncle Paul, a widower, was right after she and Larry were married.

She put that box aside. Maybe Beth Ann had sisters or nieces who would want to see the contents of these boxes. Sarah's mind was occupied with thinking of all the ways she could search for Beth Ann's relatives when it hit her; maybe she wouldn't be alive to give anything away.

Her empty stomach hurt.

Beth Ann must have been a packrat because many more boxes contained only her belongings. One even had a wedding dress all rolled up lovingly in some kind of gauze. By the time the smell of brewing coffee drifted under her locked door, one whole corner of the bedroom was filled with boxes of Beth Ann's things.

Although she was expecting it, she still jumped when someone knocked on her door. It was Sammy's voice that warned, "Sarah, don't fight me on this. Move away from the door."

She was hungry enough to do what he had ordered. The key made a grating sound as it turned in the lock. He pushed the door open just wide enough for him place a tray of food on the floor. Without saying another word, he pulled the door shut and Sarah winced once again at the sound of the key turning in the lock.

CHAPTER 42

"LET ME GET THIS RIGHT," said Tom, trying to keep his face straight. "You have a theory that Lucky found the source of the scent he smells on the floor."

The small group, made up of Joe, Clara, Tom, and Mitch were in the office staring at the stain, daring it to give up its secret. Lucky was sniffing it. "And," Tom continued, choking back his amusement, "the reason he won't go inside is because he's waiting for that person to come back to town."

Clara nodded her head.

Getting Lucky to leave his outside guarding position and the even bigger struggle of dragging him into the real estate office had worn out Joe. His urging Lucky to go inside for another whiff of Sammy's calling card was the only reason Lucky had given up his vigilance.

Patiently, Clara repeated her reasons for thinking the unkempt stranger had to be Sammy. Mitch and Tom listened, and they had to agree that some of it made sense. The worker that showed up last November to work at Sarah Blakeman's vineyard fit into the time line, but that didn't mean he was Sammy.

Mitch watched Lucky as he sniffed the dried spot of blood on the floor. "I hate to burst your bubble, Clara, but there's no way a dog can trace the smell of blood while it's inside a man's body. There has to be either dried or fresh blood on him."

"Where did you pick up that bit of information?" asked Tom.

"Remember the week I was sent to the Upper Peninsula for training? That was right before Molly and I finally worked out our misunderstandings." Everyone nodded, remembering the cookout catastrophe that had finally brought them together. "Several days of that week we spent in the field working with tracker dogs, so that's how I know."

The group was silent. Mitch had just shot down Clara's best piece of evidence.

Suddenly she pointed at Tom's finger that sported a colorful band-aid. "What's with your finger, Tom?" she asked and her eyes were alive with anticipation.

Tom shrugged. "It's a paper cut. Man, it's hard to believe that a cut that small could hurt so bad and bleed so much." He stopped talking because Clara was literally jumping up and down.

"Maybe Sammy had some blood on him! Maybe he cut himself shaving." She stopped jumping because Joe had described the man as having a hairy face. Then her face brightened. "The shoe! Sammy's shoe! Lucky snatched it off Sammy's foot the day he stabbed you, Tom! He knows what Sammy smells like!"

"Nice try," Tom said quietly as he patted her back. "There's no one who wants to catch that monster more than I do, but we need more evidence."

Joe and Clara sat quietly and watched Tom and Mitch walk out the door.

"I really don't think I'm wrong," Clara said in a subdued voice. "I wish they had taken me more seriously."

On an impulse, Joe crossed the room and hugged her. Startled, Clara jerked away. Since it had taken a long time for him to work up enough courage to do this, he held on. Blissful relief spread through him when Clara's body slowly relaxed and melted into his.

Being comforted by a hug from her best friend was nice, but it surprised her how natural it felt to hug him; she wondered why they had never tried this before.

Joe's heart was beating so hard he thought he was going to pass out.

MARIE TAPPED HER TOE impatiently on the sidewalk, but since she was still wearing her nurse's shoes, the muted sound wasn't very intimidating. In fact, it made Tom laugh.

"Give me some slack, lady! I'm only a few minutes late!" He jumped out of his car, ran around to the other side, and opened the door for Marie.

"It's not you, Tom. It's me," she said wearily. "I'm tired, I'm hungry, and my feet hurt. Are you really cooking dinner for me tonight?"

"It's happening as we speak!" boasted Tom. "Mitch and I spent time with Clara today listening to her far-out ideas about Sammy. I didn't go back to work; I went grocery shopping."

"Ah, a home-cooked meal and a foot rub! Can life get any better?" Marie murmured as she scooted as close to Tom as the seat belt allowed.

"Wait a minute! What's this foot rub bit?" laughed Tom. "Where did that come from?"

"A girl can dream, can't she?" purred Marie.

"Keep talking like that and you'll get yourself into trouble," Tom said in a husky voice.

"Who says I don't want to?" Marie's hand sneaked over to his knee.

"Cut that out," growled Tom, pushing her hand away. "You're gonna get us both killed!"

Marie laughed while retreating to her side of the car. "Just checking to see if you're still alive. Want to tell me Clara's far-out idea?"

Tom finished the story as they pulled into his driveway. Marie remained seated even after he had done the polite thing and opened her door. “Come on, Marie, get out, or have you changed your mind about eating my cooking?”

“No, I’m just thinking,” Marie said as she smiled up at him and climbed out. “Clara has some good points in that theory of hers. I don’t think it’s all that far-out.”

“Really? I’m surprised. I thought they would make you laugh,” Tom said as he opened the door to his house and stopped dead in his tracks. The smell of something burning was not a good indicator that all was well for the promised dinner.

“Oh, oh,” exclaimed Marie.

Tom ran to the kitchen and threw open the oven door. Both of them stood in silence looking at the charred remains of something.

Almost reverently, Marie said, “And I thought the hospital was the only place in town that served mystery meat.”

Because she couldn’t hold it back any longer, she snickered. His reaction to her comment and snicker was instant; he was offended. How could she be so unfeeling? How would she feel if this was happening to her? A feeling of resentment was slowly building up inside him. By this time, Marie had almost collapsed from laughing. He took another look at the burned mess in the oven and decided that maybe the situation was a little funny. Eventually they both were laughing so hard they had to hang onto each other for support.

“Well,” said Tom, wiping the tears off his face, “what do you suggest we do now?”

“What else did you have planned for dinner? Some side dish like a salad or potatoes? Perhaps dessert?” she asked hopefully.

“I hadn’t really thought past the meat course, which, by the way, was a beef roast. But I do have dessert!”

“Something you whipped up all by yourself?”

"Well, I bought it and brought it home. Does that count?"

"Depends on what it is," she teased.

"A pecan pie," he proudly proclaimed as he removed it from the store-box.

Marie's eyes lighted up. "My all-time favorite pie! What a lucky choice!"

"Luck had nothing to do with it. Remember my meeting with Clara today? I asked her what you liked and she told me about your lifelong love of pecan pie."'

"Then I think for dinner I would settle for a cup of coffee and a piece of that pie, *if* a foot rub was included on the menu," she concluded.

"You've got it. I'll even throw in a scoop of ice cream for the pie."

"Be still, my heart," Marie laughed. She quickly sobered up as she remembered something she wanted to tell him. "Tom, remember the Church Lady!"

"How could I forget?" Tom answered, as he plugged in the coffee maker.

"She was released from the hospital when it was determined that all she had was a hard bump on her head. But today she came back to the hospital especially to see me. I guess it's because she found out that I'm engaged to a policeman. She wanted to tell someone about, and this is the word she used, her epiphany."

Tom raised his red eyebrows. "Her epiphany? She had a sudden intuitive revelation of something?" Secretly he was proud of himself for knowing the meaning of the word.

"Yes. It has to do with the man who escaped. From the very first time she laid eyes on him she felt as if she had seen him before. It bugged her the entire time they sang together in jail, but she never could figure it out until she had her epiphany."

“Are you going to tell me her intuitive revelation or am I just going to stand here and listen to this long story while the ice cream melts?”

“Be patient. She has a name, but I always think of her as the Church Lady. Anyhow, she truly lives up to that name. She’s involved with all kinds of activities in the church, and one of them is the Newcomer’s Club. New members of the church are thrown together and pretty soon they don’t feel like new members any more. One couple that joined a few years ago was Larry and Sarah Blakeman. They inherited a vineyard out on the peninsula from his Uncle Paul who died quiet unexpectedly. The Church Lady got to know them quite well before Larry, too, died quite suddenly.”

“I haven’t heard the epiphany yet,” complained Tom.

“Here it is. The prisoner and Larry, according to her, are one and the same.”

“Wait a minute!” Tom was stunned to silence for a moment as he waved the ice cream scooper through the air. “She didn’t have an epiphany, she had a delusion! You just told me Larry’s dead.”

“She was so upset by what you called her ‘intuitive revelation’ that she looked up the church record of his funeral and even went to the cemetery to make sure he had a grave and a marker.”

“Pray tell, Marie, what am I supposed to make of this?” Tom pleaded.

Marie laughed. “I have no idea. Aren’t we all supposed to have a double somewhere in the world?”

Tom thought for a moment. “I’ve heard that saying, but there’s nothing that says your double would show up in your home town. But you know something? I just had an epiphany of my own.”

“Is this epiphany thing contagious? Am I going to have one next?” she giggled as she covered her head as protection to ward one off. “So are you going to share yours with me?”

"It's not really an epiphany that I had, but I just like to say that word," Tom grinned. "But this is the second time today that I've heard about the vineyard that is now owned by Sarah, the widow of Larry. Does that count as at least an eyebrow raiser if it's not an epiphany?"

"Consider my eyebrows raised. Why did you hear about it before?"

"It was part of Clara's theory. I didn't tell you the name of the person who owned the vineyard where the scruffy man works, but it's owned by Sarah Blakeman."

"Do you believe in coincidences?" Marie asked quietly. "I don't."

"Come on, now. You can't believe this Sammy thing and that vineyard are connected!"

"Why can't I? I think you and Mitch brushed Clara's theory away too soon."

"Know what I think?" When Marie didn't answer, he told her anyway. "I think you should stick to your profession, and I'll stick to mine."

Marie's head jerked up, a sharp reply on her tongue, ready to challenge Tom. Watching her face, he knew he had crossed the line. Before she could say anything, he held up both hands and said one word.

"Sorry."

Her mouth snapped shut.

Picking up her fork, she resumed eating her piece of pecan pie that, come to think of it, wasn't her favorite after all.

TOM WAS SURPRISED THE next day to get a call from Mitch. "Something up, buddy?" he asked.

"I've been thinking. Maybe we brushed Clara's theory off too soon," Mitch admitted. "How do you feel about it?"

"She has some valid points, I agree."

"Any point in particular?" asked Mitch.

Tom replied slowly. "Remember how we laughed when Lucky carried Sammy's shoe around? If anyone knows how Sammy smells, it's Lucky!"

"That's the strongest point of her argument. But on what grounds can we investigate?"

Tom thought a moment. "I suppose it wouldn't hurt to send a car out there but without a search warrant we wouldn't accomplish much."

"When would we do it?" Mitch asked. "Tomorrow's Sunday and I think the girls are planning something, but I don't know what."

"Yeah, there's been a lot of telephoning back and forth. Let's talk about this tomorrow."

"You mean after we find out what they're planning? Sounds good to me, but if something's going on out there, I hope we're not too late," a worried Mitch said as the call ended.

CHAPTER 43

SAMMY FOUND CLARENCE and Albert waiting for him at the bottom of the stairs. "Don't get your shorts all in a ball," he snarled at them. "I didn't do nothin' bad to her!"

"But you said you was goin' to," Clarence looked at Albert for confirmation. "Didn't he, Albert?" Albert, who had been prepared to stop Sammy if he had carried out the plan he had concocted at breakfast, was so relieved he couldn't speak. He just nodded his head in affirmation.

"I didn't say *when* I was gonna do it, now did I?" Sammy snarled.

"Have you really thought this through?" Albert asked timidly. Always afraid of getting out of character of the person he was pretending to be since joining the gang, he hesitated to show too much knowledge about anything; his tutors and professors at the university wouldn't recognize him now.

"What do I have to think through? It's simple," Sammy smiled as he explained. "We get rid of Sarah and then we own the vineyard, get it?"

"But Sammy, you can't own the vineyard if Sarah doesn't sign it over to you, and how are you goin' to get her to do that?" Realizing what he had just said, Albert blanched. He had seen some of Sammy's methods of persuasion.

"Humm. You have a point. Maybe we could say she went back home to her family and hired us to run the vineyard." He thought a bit and then smiled. "Yeah, I like that better than tryin' to get her to sign somethin'. It's less messy."

Clarence and Albert visibly relaxed.

Sammy bristled. "I saw that! You two are nothing but lily-white choirboys sweet on Sarah; I can see it in your faces! Just remember what I told you before. I have no qualms about *getting' rid of her along with any of her close friends*!" He held their gaze until both men nodded, indicating that they understood the situation. "Now," he said, convinced he had everything under his control, "back to work."

"To do what?" asked Clarence. "Did Sarah tell you what we needed to do?"

"We don't need Sarah no more. Remember all those books I read? I know more about how to run a vineyard than Sarah ever did."

"So what do we do?" Clarence asked again.

"We mow between the rows and pull weeds. Pretty simple, wouldn't you say? Runnin' a vineyard ain't rocket science!" Sammy said disdainfully as he led them out the door.

SARAH PRESSED HER EAR to the door after Sammy had pulled it shut. Faintly hearing Albert and Clarence's voices did nothing to calm her fears. Whatever was going on, it was obvious that all three were in this together. Her one hope, and now she realized it was naïve of her to even think it, was that either Clarence or Albert would step in and stop Sammy from doing anything bad to her.

She gave up trying to hear what they were saying, picked up the tray and carried it to her desk. Whether it was the cook or the hunger that made the food taste so good, Sarah didn't care. She scraped every dish clean, wondering how she could even have an appetite.

While passing a mirror on her way to place the tray by the door, she caught a glimpse of herself. Startled at her unkempt reflection, her first thought, *I don't want to die with dirty hair*, was so morbid she almost laughed. After a hot shower, she felt better. Brushing her teeth and applying a little lip-gloss paid off in renewed energy to once again tackle the contents of the boxes that were still in the storage area.

For the next hour she followed Uncle Paul's journey as he graduated from law school and went on to Detroit where he gained partnership in a large firm.

Uncle Paul had gone into politics! It was with growing interest that she traced the path of Paul Blakeman as he steadily progressed from local and state elected positions to one at the national level. Why hadn't Larry ever mentioned this? He had to have been aware of an uncle who was constantly mentioned in the media.

Her thoughts were interrupted by a knock on the door. Startled, she glanced at the clock and saw that it was lunchtime. The morning had gone by so quickly. Sammy again gave her the curt command to stand back from the door; she did. The key grated in the lock and the door opened. His arms reached in, retrieved the empty breakfast tray, and replaced it with the loaded luncheon one: a bowl of soup and a sandwich.

CHAPTER 44

CLARENCE WAS WASHING the lunch dishes while listening to Albert and Sammy's heated conversation. They were still sitting around the table nursing cold cups of coffee.

Sammy was trying to talk Albert into changing his appearance so that he eventually could go into town without being recognized. He would never admit this to Albert, but he had long suspected that Albert was smarter than he let on. When it came time to harvest the grapes and market them, Sammy needed someone shrewd enough to hold his own in a competitive market.

"You want me to do what?" Clarence heard Albert bellow. "Hell, no!"

Clarence scampered back to the table. "What's he want you to do?" he asked breathlessly.

Albert jumped out of his chair so abruptly it toppled back and crashed to the floor. "Sammy wants me to shave my head!" he yelled.

"Oh, listen to the little prissy-pretty boy!" mocked Sammy. "Ain't his hair just precious?" His tone changed. "Get this straight, Albert. I took you in, I gave you a place to hide from the cops, I clothed and fed you, and now when I ask you to do one little thing to make life easier and safer for all of us, you pull this girlie stuff on me."

Albert hung his head.

"And here's something else I'm gonna do just for good measure," Sammy added disdainfully. "I'm gonna change the color of your hair."

Clarence snickered. Albert gave him a dirty look before replying to Sammy while touching his forehead where the black hair grew down to a point. "Tell me, smarty, how you gonna hide my widow's peak? How many men do you know who has one of these?"

Sammy sarcastically replied, "Only one other guy, and he's dead. I'm talkin' about Larry if you didn't follow my drift."

"I followed it all right," Albert replied. "Anyhow, even shaving my head, you can't get rid of it."

"When your hair is black, I agree it would stick out like a sore thumb," Sammy snickered, "but wait until you're a blond! No one will notice your widow's peak."

It was very quiet in the kitchen. Clarence tried to break the heavy silence by banging some pans together, but nothing worked. Sammy and Albert were battling it out without saying a word.

Albert sighed and gave in. "Guess it won't hurt. Go ahead and do it," he said quietly.

Sammy gave a triumphant little snort as he left to go upstairs to get his electric razor. When he passed Sarah's locked room, he fleetingly wondered how she was passing the time.

The feeling of having power over others made him smile when he returned to the kitchen and saw Albert sitting in a chair with a dishtowel draped around his shoulder. He was still leader of this crew and they had better not forget it! He was smiling as he shaved Albert's head; Albert wasn't.

Clarence tried to keep a straight face, but every time he looked at the freshly shaved head of his friend, laughter bubbled up and spilled out. "Clarence, I'm gonna bust your balls if you don't cut that out!" Albert warned.

"I can't help it!" Clarence gasped. "Go look at yourself in the mirror and then I'll bet you laugh, too!"

It was a roar, not laughter that came out of the bathroom.

"You son of a bitch, Sammy! I've a mind to…" He stopped in mid-sentence when he felt the sharp point of Sammy's knife poking him in the back.

"That'll be enough out of you," Sammy said quietly, letting the knife send the message. "Now you and Clarence be good little boys. Go to the vineyard and finish up with the mowin' and weedin' we started yesterday. And, while I'm gone, if I find that either one of you visits our little princess upstairs you will become better acquainted with this," he said, waving the knife. "Understand?"

Both men nodded their heads.

Clarence worked up enough nerve to ask, "Where you goin'?"

"I'm goin' into town! Seems I have to buy some blond hair color." He smirked as he looked at Albert. "I'm not finished with you yet."

A subdued Albert and Clarence got ready to go to the vineyard.

Sammy crawled into the old pick-up and headed for town.

STANDING OUTSIDE THE fire station, Joe was watching Lucky's curious behavior as the dog ate his midday treat. Lucky had not deserted his surveillance of the street since the day he had sniffed the scruffy man. Joe had moved the dog's sleeping pad and bowls outside. Lucky was cautiously eating, but he never relaxed his vigilance.

Joe shook his head in both amusement and wonder. Whatever was going through this dog's head was a mystery to everyone but Clara. She was still holding on to her ridiculous idea that Lucky had found the source of the blood on the office floor.

Since it was time for Lucky's walk, Joe snapped the leash onto his new collar that read MY NAME IS LUCKY. The collar was a gift from the owner of a shop they walked past every day. The two of them stepped out smartly, heading in the direction of Clara's office. If she wasn't busy, sometimes she would walk with them. Since that trial hug, Joe had sneaked in several more; Clara hadn't refused any of them.

They got as far as the middle of the block when Lucky froze. He stopped so quickly that Joe almost stumbled over him. A low growl started in Lucky's chest and grew louder as Joe looked around trying to find the cause of this unusual behavior.

It was quiet in town today; the sidewalks were relatively empty. Across the street Joe saw what had caught Lucky's attention. Standing outside the drug store, holding his recent purchase, was the scruffy stranger.

The leash was jerked out of Joe's hand before he was fully aware of the situation. Lucky ran faster than a dog his size should be able to run. Across the street he streaked, horns honking and brakes screeching, to arrive on the other side to find his prey had sprinted to an old truck and was already pulling into traffic. Joe arrived, puffing and, with the help of the chain, pulled Lucky back onto the sidewalk.

Joe and Lucky continued their walk, but he knew he had to stop at Clara's office to tell her she was right. Lucky had truly found the blood source.

CHAPTER 45

SARAH WAS STILL HUNGRY after eating the meager lunch, but she doubted there was anyone who would listen to her complaint. Looking out the window, she saw Sammy driving away in the old truck while Albert and Clarence were heading for the vineyard. Turning away from the window, she did a double take. There was something strange about Albert's head. Was he covering it with something white? Squinting, she finally figured out what it was; a shaved head. Now what was all that about? Shaking her head in resignation, she knew whatever it was, she probably wouldn't live long enough to find out.

That thought sent her back to the boxes. At least, looking through all that old junk, and that's what most of it was, kept her mind from dwelling on her situation.

Looking for one with the least amount of dust on the top, she hauled a box out to the middle of the bedroom. Sitting on the floor Indian style, she felt a quickening of her pulse as she viewed the contents. Old newspapers were on top. Thinking they were just fillers, she was tossing them aside until one headline caught her eye: "Congressman Paul Blakeman Caught in Double Life". The picture under the headline must have been an old promotional one, because it was of a smiling, beaming man. A politician does not smile and beam when he's been caught living a lie.

She read the articles with interest. Paul had two families; one with Beth Ann in Michigan and one with another woman in an adjoining state. How his carefully built house of cards had come tumbling down was still a mystery because no matter how hard she searched, none of the saved papers broached the subject. The last paper reported on page three that Congressman Blakeman had resigned. According to the article, the retired Congressman stated that he and his wife, Beth Ann, would be spending their time at their newly purchased vineyard in northern Michigan.

Now, Sarah knew why Uncle Paul had gone from politics to being a vintner. Yawning, she realized that most of the afternoon was gone. Since it wasn't dinnertime yet, she felt tired; a little nap would fit right into her schedule. What schedule? Who was she fooling? She was living on borrowed time, and she knew it. As she gathered up the scattered newspapers to put them back into the box, she noticed something stuck to the inside. Curiosity put the nap on hold.

The ordinary white envelope had Larry's name on it. She had become familiar with Uncle Paul's handwriting, so she was sure it was he who had addressed the envelope. Feeling as if she were invading Larry's privacy, she slowly slit the seal and unfolded a letter. It was handwritten and, from the date at the top, she figured that he had written it a few weeks after their visit to the vineyard. She held the letter in shaking hands and read:

Dear Larry,

If you are reading this, then I am dead. I had wanted to talk to you while I was alive so I could look you in the eye while I tried to explain the mess I made in the part of my life that involved you.

You see, Larry, you are my son. If that's not shocking enough, now I must tell you that you have an identical twin brother.

It all started to go wrong after my marriage to Beth Ann had become routine. Then, while I was at a political convention, I met a most willing lady.

It was all very exciting, as most affairs are. I thought I was getting away with having Lois, for that was her name, in one state and Beth Ann in another. Politically, I knew it would be suicide if I were to be found out, but I thought I was clever enough not to have that happen. I bought Lois a house in a good neighborhood, and since Beth Ann was used to my traveling for political reasons, she never questioned my absences and the extra expense.

Eventually, I was found out. Bad public opinion would never let me get elected again, so I resigned. Poor Beth Ann was humiliated. I will regret to the day I die hurting that good lady, because I did love her.

It took some time for her to forgive me. For a while, she resisted my attempts to get back into her good graces, but eventually, she came around. I was devastated when she died a few years later.

Beth Ann had just taken me back when the next shoe fell. Lois, in a panic, contacted me when her doctor told her she was three months pregnant.

I unraveled. I couldn't let Beth Ann, who had never been able to conceive, learn that I had fathered a child with Lois. I knew that would be the end of the marriage.

So here's when the third shoe dropped; Lois gave birth to identical twins. One baby, with my support, Lois felt she could handle. But not two. How I managed to keep all that was going on from Beth Ann, I don't know. Lois was demanding things over the phone while I was trying to figure out what to do hundreds of miles away. It was when she told me that she had put one of the twins up for adoption that I knew what I had to do. Since

I couldn't ask Beth Ann to take such a baby, my thoughts went to my brother, the man you called Dad. You must believe that my brother and his wife welcomed you into their lives with love. You grew up as their son, and I was the uncle who was always there for every one of your milestones. I paid your college tuition, I bought you your first car, and I loved you like a son, but from a distance. You were never adopted; you just became a part of their family.

Beth Ann died before she had the chance to meet the lovely woman you married. I'm sure she would have loved Sarah. I had planned on taking you aside and telling you this sordid story when the two of you spent your honeymoon here at the vineyard. But you were so happy, I lost my nerve. I'm sorry you have to learn all of this after I'm gone because I know you have a million questions.

Somewhere there is another you. Lois named the one she kept 'Albert' after her own dad. There's a saying that somewhere in the world everyone has a look-alike. But in your case, you really do.

Only in this letter can I call you son. That forbidden word has haunted me all the years I watched you grow up. It cut like a knife when I heard you calling someone else Dad, even though that man was my own brother.

So now you know the whole story. Please don't hate me for my weakness, because that weakness produced you; somewhere Albert is living a full life. I made sure he was well provided for by investments I made for Lois. She has had the means to live a life of relative leisure, with ample money to support both of them. I never heard from her again.

I write this with such love in my heart for you. Take care of the vineyard and think of me when the grapes are purple and full of juice.

Your dad,

Paul Blakeman

Sarah sat, too stunned to move. Recent images reeled through her mind. From the first time she laid eyes on Albert walking down her driveway to the scene in the vineyard that brought everything to a head, her heart had known. Albert was Larry's mirror image. She had not admitted this before, but now it didn't seem to matter anymore; she no longer thought of Larry when she looked at Albert.

Sarah had held herself so rigidly while reading the letter her body protested when she dragged herself to her feet. What was she supposed to do with this information? Take it to the grave with her? That somehow didn't seem quite right; Albert had a right to know. The idea of a nap was out of the question; her mind now spun in different directions, making her dizzy. She ran to the window. It was the only escape out of this room, but once again, she came to the same conclusion; she would never survive the drop.

In the distance, she saw Albert and Clarence trudging back from the vineyard. On an impulse, she grabbed a hand mirror and ran back to the window. It was late afternoon, but there was enough sun to capture it on the mirror and reflect it. Talking, the two men didn't see the flash from the window, but a lucky aim sent the flash into Albert's eye. Startled he looked up, saw her in the window, and waved. Now what should she do? How could she get a message to him? She tried pantomiming. Putting her fingers on her lips, she then pointed them at Albert. He threw her a kiss. No, no, she shook her head. He held up his hands and shrugged. What? Frantically she grabbed a tablet and a pencil and pretended to write. He shook his head, yes. He understood that. Now what?

She saw Clarence nudge Albert; Sammy was coming down the driveway in the old truck. What if he had seen Albert looking up at her window? Her heart sank and all hope fled. There was no way she was going to get out of this alive.

To Paul and his two sons, she whispered, “I’m sorry.”

CHAPTER 46

THE HEAVY SILENCE IN the office of Allen Real Estate reflected the seriousness of the subject being discussed. Clara was the first to speak. “Now what?”

Joe, who had just described Lucky’s second encounter with the scruffy man to her, shook his head. “You heard Tom and Mitch. They laughed at your Sammy theory, so we know we can’t go to them.”

Clara made a face.

“We also have no business taking this on ourselves,” Joe repeated for the umpteenth time. “We’re talking about a really bad guy who is fast with a knife. So what if we prove that the scruffy guy is Sammy if we get killed in the process? Huh? Answer me that!”

“There is no answer, Joe, but there’s something else that’s been bothering me.”

“The Nancy Drew syndrome again?” Joe managed a smile.

“I knew I never should have told you about my girlhood hero!” Clara laughed as she took a playful swipe at Joe. “Now listen to this. Remember my story about the beauty shop and Betty’s no-show? Betty was surprised when Sarah didn’t show up to get her hair cut because she had been so pleased that Betty had an opening.”

“Oh, oh. I can see where you’re going with this. You see a maiden in distress! Not only that, she’s a maiden that only the two of us can rescue from the clutches of the evil Sammy!”

“Don’t be such a smart ass, Joe! But yes, that’s what I see. The day she was in the beauty shop was the day all hell broke loose. After I had informed the women that Sammy's car had been found, I heard her ask Betty when Sammy had disappeared, what part of his body had been wounded, and what did he look like. She acted like a woman who had just learned something very disturbing. Maybe she had just realized that the guy working at her vineyard was Sammy. Anyhow, the last I saw of her was when she threw two twenties down on the counter and ran out of the shop."

"Are you thinking that if she went home and confronted him with the fact that she knew who he was, her life would be in danger?"

"Well, what do you think? Life in that house sure wouldn't be all fun and games anymore!" Clara's face brightened. "You know, I haven't visited a working vineyard in years! Aren't there tours that take tourists around that area?"

"Yes, there are wine-tasting tours, but they only stop where the wine is actually made. Sarah's vineyard just grows the grapes to sell to the winemakers. Tours wouldn't stop there…even by accident, if that's how your brain is working."

"Rats."

Joe got up to leave. "Did I tell you that the old fire truck is finally fixed?"

"About time", answered Clara. "Who finally figured out what was wrong with it?"

"It was just a combination of a lot of mechanics' opinions, but we're pretty sure we've solved the problem. I get to take it out on a test run tomorrow."

"Uh, Joe, where do you think you will be going on this test run?" she asked. "Any chance it could be a drive up the peninsula?"

"No, and I don't like the direction this conversation is going! Just drop it!"

"But Joe," she pleaded. "What about Lucky? He's the one who figured this thing out! He's the only one who can recognize Sammy and the fire truck is the only thing he'll ride on!"

"Clara," Joe replied impatiently. "Just forget we ever had this conversation."

"I'll pack a picnic basket, and when we get to the vineyard we can stop and say we are lost, and accidentally Lucky can get loose and run off…." Clara purred as she batted her eyes and snuggled close to Joe

"Oh no you don't, Clara! Don't pull that seductive act on me! There's no way in hell I'm going near that vineyard without some kind of back-up."

"Wouldn't Lucky and I count?" she cooed as she kissed him on the neck.

"Cut that out! Come on, Lucky, let's get out of here before she talks us into doing something that will get us all killed!"

"Think about it, Joe!" she called to him as he and Lucky rushed to the door.

Joe stopped, turned around, and winked seductively. "Feel free to kiss me on the neck anytime you want!" he whispered.

Clara laughed and blew him a kiss.

SAMMY THREW OPEN THE door of the old truck and angrily yelled at Clarence and Albert who he had just caught waving to Sarah. "That's it! You two have just signed her death warrant! I can't take the chance that one of you will do somethin' stupid and get us all exposed."

He looked at Clarence's anguished face. "I know you're sweet on her, both of you. The two of you are nothin' but chicken-livered girly men! But don't worry, I won't tell you when I'm gonna do it. I'll just tell you about it in the mornin'." Sammy gave an evil chuckle as he walked away.

"What are we gonna do, Albert?" Clarence frantically asked when Sammy got out of earshot. "Are we really gonna let him kill Sarah?"

Albert was thinking fast. "Little buddy, how good an actor do you think you could be if you knew you could save her life?"

"Since I ain't never acted before, I guess I don't know."

"You have to think hard about what I'm gonna ask you to do, because a lot depends on it."

"Come on, Albert, you're scaring me. What if I can't act? What happens?"

"Then Sammy will kill all three of us."

Clarence's face turned white. "Oh, my! I-I-I'm one of the three?"

"Yes, Clarence, you're one of the three that Sammy will kill if we screw this up. But if we don't do nothin'…."

Clarence took a deep breath. "Okay, I'll do it. I'll try *real* hard, but talk slow."

"If this is gonna work you'd better be aimin' to win an Oscar," Albert whispered.

Clarence looked puzzled. "Who's Oscar?

"Forget I said that. Now listen closely…."

CHAPTER 47

SARAH'S STOMACH GROWLED. It was long past dinnertime but no food had been delivered to her room. With growing dread she realized what that meant. If he were going to kill her tonight, why would it matter if she died hungry? Sammy probably regarded it as a thrifty way to save food.

Trying to hold down the panic, she paced. What do you do with the last few hours you have left? Think about the life you have lived up to this point starting with early memories of childhood? The faces of her mom and dad flashed through her mind. If there really is a Heaven, would she get to see them? Would they recognize her as a grown woman? Pray. She needed to pray and ask for forgiveness of her sins. What sins? Desperately trying to think of a sin that she could petition God to forgive, she became aware of a familiar smell that was coming from downstairs. It wasn't the smell of food cooking…but what was it? A memory from the beauty shop surfaced; it was the chemical smell of a hair product! First Albert's shaved head, and now this. What was going on? She shrugged; what was the use of wasting time trying to figure that one out?

Finally, at midnight she said her last prayer, shed her last tear, whispered to Larry that she would see him soon and stretched out on the bed.

It was two o'clock when the tapping sound fitted into her dream. Albert, standing on a tall ladder outside her window, was frantically trying to tap loudly enough to wake Sarah but not loudly enough to alert Sammy. Clarence had pulled off his first acting job like a pro but the pills obviously hadn't been sleeping pills.

The idea, a good one even though it hadn't worked, had been to put Sammy out of commission. Albert knew his life wouldn't be worth a plugged nickel if he were caught rescuing Sarah. Desperate to get to her before Sammy did, he tapped harder. He saw Sarah stir and turn over. "No, no! Sarah, for God's sake, wake up!"

It took a hard tap to arouse Sarah. Confused, she sat up in bed and looked toward the door, fully expecting to see Sammy standing there with the knife in his hand that would end her life. Another tap and a glance at the window struck a spark of hope in her heart. Maybe all was not lost; someone was coming to rescue her. Rushing to the window, she saw an Albert peering in at her who no longer looked like Larry.

Sarah threw open the window and Albert stepped off the ladder into the room. Putting his fingers over his lips, he motioned for her to be silent.

Pantomiming, he demonstrated to her that she needed to get dressed. Nodding, she grabbed her clothes from yesterday's pile and ran into the bathroom. Coming out fully dressed, she accepted the jacket he handed to her. Looking down at her feet, he shook his head and pointed to his own. She understood he was telling her that she was going to need more than the sandals she was wearing.

Showing her that they needed a flashlight was a bit harder but she finally figured out what he was telling her; she handed him one. Finally ready, he was rushing her towards the window when she remembered the letter. She held up a finger asking for a moment, ran to the desk and grabbed it. Searching her clothes for a pocket and finding none, she handed the letter to him. He understood. Taking the letter from her, he shoved it into his pocket, completely unaware that the letter contained information that would change his life.

At the last minute, he turned back. Even in the dark, he had been able to see the boxes stacked in the corner. He quickly moved Beth Ann's treasures to the middle of the floor and piled the pillows on the bed to make a mound to resemble Sarah's body. With luck, maybe when Sammy was sneaking into the dark room, he would fall over the boxes in his eagerness to stab the pillows. Albert almost laughed aloud at his little trap.

Sarah was already out the window and halfway down by the time Albert pulled the window shut. At the bottom, they both silently grabbed the ladder and moved it back from the house. Albert took her hand.

As they started to run into the darkness, the light came on in Sarah's room. If they had wasted time to turn around, they would have seen Sammy's furious face at the window.

IT WAS THE THUMP, followed by a string of swear words that woke Clarence. He cringed to think of what was probably happening in Sarah's bedroom.

He hesitated for a moment, not sure if his acting ability would get him through the next scene. Albert had told him how to behave when Sammy accused him of being in on Sarah's rescue. "Act surprised," Albert had said. "Act hurt that he could even think you'd do something like this. And you better be good, because your life depends on it."

Clarence groaned, rolled over, and decided to stay in bed. Let Sammy find him asleep. How could he be in on the plot if he was sound asleep?

Pulling the covers over his head, he tried to get his mind off the punishment that awaited him if Sammy thought he was part of the escape plan. The fact that he had been able to pull a fast one on Sammy made him smile.

He had actually enjoyed play-acting last night at dinner. The plot that Albert had dreamed up in desperation had worked. Clarence had mentioned right before dinner that if he ever got back into civilization, he would like to follow up on his ambition to become a waiter in a fancy restaurant so he could pocket all the big tips the millionaires left.

Albert's planned reaction to this announcement was to hoot, laugh, and state that Clarence was much too dumb to become such a waiter. Sammy had looked on in amusement for a while, but finally he joined Albert.

Challenged, Clarence draped a towel over one arm and ushered Albert and Sammy to their seats at the table. He haughtily stated that he would prepare their plates and serve them individually the way they do in a fancy restaurant. That left him alone in the kitchen to carry out Albert's plan.

In the small bath off the kitchen, there were two plain bottles of pills in the cabinet. There were no labels on the bottles but there was a good chance that one of them might contain sleeping pills. For good measure, Clarence took five from each bottle, smashed them, and dropped them into hot gravy where they dissolved. With much pomposity, he marched from the kitchen with two loaded plates in his hands. Very carefully, he served the intended one to Sammy. Clarence's presentation was applauded and the meal progressed.

All evening long, both men watched Sammy, hoping to see some signs that one of the pills was working. By bedtime, Albert realized that his plot to put Sammy out of commission hadn't worked. Rescuing Sarah was going to be as life threatening to him as it was for her. If caught, he had no doubt that Sammy would kill them both without batting an eye.

CLARENCE HAD MANAGED to doze off again. When Sammy threw open the bedroom door and rushed into his room Clarence honestly looked startled and, therefore, quite innocent. “What th..!” he grumbled.

“Get out of that bed you ungrateful worm! I know you’re in on this!”

“In on what?” Clarence remembered to look surprised.

“Sarah’s missin’! And don’t you play ignorant with me!”

“She’s missin’? You didn’t lock her door? It’s your fault if you didn’t, you know. You can’t blame that on me!”

“Oh shut up! You know I locked her door!” Sammy was looking agitated and it had nothing to do with the missing Sarah.

“So how did she get out then? Fly?” Clarence snickered a bit.

“I’m goin’ to the bathroom, and I want you up and dressed when I get back! Hear me?”

Clarence watched Sammy run out of the room and then he heard the bathroom door slam shut. The toilet flushed once, the toilet flushed again, and it flushed one more time before Sammy reappeared in Clarence’s room.

“Get your ass movin’! She can’t be too far away since sissies can’t run very fast. We’ll find them!”

“Them?” asked Clarence innocently. “Who’s them?”

“You don’t think she climbed out that window all by herself do you? Your old buddy Albert is missing, too.” Sammy was looking agitated again. “Go down and make some coffee. I’m goin’ to the bathroom.”

Sammy looked rather haggard when he entered the kitchen. Clarence handed him a cup of coffee. “Ready?” he asked.

“As soon as I make another trip to the bathroom! What was in that food you served last night?” he called over his shoulder as he ran down the hall.

Clarence smiled. Now he knew what was in one of the bottles in the small bathroom; Old Sammy was feeling the effect of five laxatives. The idea hadn't been a complete failure because the laxatives were doing a good job of slowing Sammy down. He wasn't going to be too far away from a commode for the next few hours.

Seeing his chance to get away, Clarence yelled down the hall where he could see Sammy hustle into the bathroom again, "I'm startin' without you!"

He didn't wait around for a response.

CHAPTER 48

DAWN WAS NOTHING BUT a promise in the eastern sky when an exhausted Albert and Sarah, drained from hours of running and fast walking, felt safe enough to stop. The sound of their wheezing was covered by traffic noise from the nearby road.

"What are the odds that a motorist would pick us up?" gasped Albert who was holding his side. "I'm thinkin' about standin' along the side of the road and puttin' out my thumb."

Sarah, panting, shook her head. "What are the odds that Frank's not driving the truck right now waiting for us to be stupid enough to do that?" Seeing Albert's hurt face, she added quickly while wiping the sweat off her brow, "Albert, I'm sorry. I didn't mean to say you're stupid. I just don't think it's a smart thing to do."

"So we're goin' to town? Is that your plan?" Albert felt sick inside. The last thing he wanted to do was to tell Sarah he couldn't show his face in town. How would she treat him when she found out he was the escaped prisoner?

Sarah was staring at him intently. Remembering his changed appearance, he blushed and ran his hand over his orange stubby hair. "Frank sure did a number on me, didn't he?" he asked ruefully.

Sarah nodded. "You might look different, but you're still the Albert who I know is somehow connected to Frank; that means you aren't a choir boy. So it puzzles me that you defied Sammy the Grunt, because I know that's who he is. You kept him from killing me."

Albert choked, "Y-y-you knew?"

"Yes, I knew who he was but you haven't answered my question."

"Sarah," Albert looked at her intently, "Do you know Sammy would have killed you in a minute if he thought you knew?"

"I figured as much. He was determined to own my vineyard, one way or another." She stepped closer to Albert, looked into his eyes, and asked again, "Why did you risk your life to save me?"

Now was not the time for a full confession. Shuffling his feet, he looked down at the ground and mumbled his answer. "It just didn't seem right, Sarah. I figured you were worth savin' even if I got killed doin' it."

"Thank you, thank you, thank you!" she fervently kissed him on the cheek. "There are no other words that can express my gratitude! And we know he will kill us both if he finds us." Sarah thought about the letter in Albert's pocket. She hesitated sharing the letter with him so soon, but the thought that they might be caught made the decision for her. If Albert was going to die trying to save her, the least she could do for him was share the letter's information. "Uh, Albert, you remember seeing all those boxes in my room?"

He laughed. "Did you see me move 'em to the middle of the floor? I figured Sammy would stumble over 'em on his way to stab your pillows!"

"Stab my pillows?"

"Yeah. I made a mound out of your pillows that are probably nothing but feathers by now."

"Ouch!" She shuddered. "That's a pretty gruesome picture!"

"Sammy is a pretty gruesome man."

Sarah took a deep breath, rubbed the goose bumps from her arms, and continued. "Anyhow, back to the boxes. Since I had nothing else to do, I started going through old boxes that I found in a storage area. Most of them were filled with junk because I suspect Uncle Paul's wife, Beth Ann, was something of a packrat."

"So is my mom," Albert commented softly.

Sarah, realizing that Albert had just given her an opening, asked, "Is your mom's name Lois?"

Albert jerked as if he'd been shot. "Where the hell did that come from?" he demanded. Wild-eyed, he jumped to his feet. "You can't possibly know anything about my mother!"

"Calm down, Albert," she patted the grass beside her. "Sit here; I have a story you need to hear."

Leery as he was even to talk about his mother, curiosity got the upper hand; he reluctantly sat down beside her. Impatiently he listened to the story, wondering how it could have anything to do with his mother. With half an ear, he paid scant attention to the mention of an Uncle Paul who had died and willed the vineyard to his nephew, Larry. He wanted to urge Sarah to hurry up and get to the part about his mother, but he held back. Maybe he wasn't going to like what she had to tell him. The story got a bit interesting when Sarah got to the part of how Uncle Paul's political career had been ruined by a scandal. Uncle Paul had lived a double life.

Sarah stopped talking to give Albert a chance to ponder how all this information had any connection to him.

Albert didn't say anything for a minute. Finally, he asked very quietly, "Does this double life thing have anything to do with Larry and me lookin' alike?"

"The whole story is in your pocket, Albert. I found a letter Paul had written to Larry right before he died. He intended Larry to find it, but after Paul died, someone just stuffed it into one of the boxes in storage. Larry never saw the letter."

Sarah got up and walked away leaving Albert alone to read the letter written by the father he had never known.

Later, thinking she'd given Albert more than enough time to read Paul's letter, she was about to walk back when the sounds of wheezing, labored breaths, and the thrashing of underbrush sent her scurrying behind a large tree. Clarence, bursting into the clearing, stopped abruptly. Seeing no one, he was about to plunge on when Sarah stepped out from the tree. "Clarence! You found us!"

"Oh, Sarah, thank God!" he cried, throwing his sweaty arms around her. "I was afraid I'd run in the wrong direction!"

Untangling his arms from her neck, she frantically looked around expecting to see Sammy running out of the woods, his knife flashing. "Where is he?"

"He ain't followin' me," Clarence panted, trying to catch his breath.

"I don't understand!" said Sarah. "You had no trouble finding us, so where's Sammy? Do you think he's changed his mind about killing me?"

"Oh, he ain't changed his mind, Sarah. But right now he's bein' kept busy doin' somethin' else." Clarence snickered.

What could he be doing that he considered more important than getting rid of her? Curious, she asked, "How did you get away from Sammy?"

He wiped the sweat off his face, took a deep breath, and decided it was time to level with Sarah. "You've been callin' him *Sammy*, so you know? You know he's Sammy the Grunt?"

"Oh, Clarence, I've known he was a bad guy since the day I got my hair cut. The whole beauty shop was talking about nothing else, and all I had to do was put the facts together to figure out the man I had taken in on a snowy November night was Sammy the Grunt."

"Boy, it's a good thing Sammy didn't know that! He would've killed you a long time ago!" Realizing how harsh that sounded, he blushed. "Well, if you found out about Sammy in the beauty shop, you must have found out that it was Albert who escaped from jail that same day."

Sarah's face turned white. Albert was the escaped prisoner? Suspiciously, she looked at Clarence. Was he the only one of the three who wasn't wanted by the police? Afraid of the answer, she asked him anyway. "And you, Clarence, are the police looking for you, too?"

When he dropped his head and wouldn't look at her, she had his answer. *My God*, she thought; *three out of three and all living under my roof.* She cringed at the realization of how naïve she had been.

Determined to survive the day, she motioned to Clarence. "Let's go find Albert."

Albert was sitting quietly under the tree, unable to move. How could this be? Of all the bad decisions he had made in his life, how had they managed to bring him to this very spot in the world, holding a letter in his hand, a letter that had been written by the man who had fathered him? It was almost too much information to absorb, but it did answer some questions. For one, the mystery of his mother's endless money supply was solved.

His head snapped up when he heard voices. Thinking Sammy had found them, he picked up a large stick and hid behind a tree. He recognized the feeling of relief that flooded him at the sight of Clarence, but that was not the entire explanation for the warmth that accompanied the relief. He was thankful that his buddy was still alive. In the back of his mind, he had written Clarence off, the victim of a frustrated Sammy. Grabbing Clarence in a bear hug, he cried, "I can't believe you're still alive! How in the world did you survive Sammy's wrath?"

Clarence fought his way out of Albert's grasp, and said haughtily, "Have you forgotten my acting ability? Oscar would have been proud of me!"

Sarah looked at Albert for help; when he just rolled his eyes and shook his head, she dropped the question.

Turning to Clarence, she asked, "But why isn't Sammy with you? You said he was busy doing something else but I'm having trouble figuring out what that could be. How did you get away from him?"

Clarence cleared his throat. "Ah, Sarah, you know the two bottles of pills you keep in the small bath off the kitchen?"

Sarah nodded. "What about those pills?"

"I think I know what was in one of the bottles," Clarence stated.

Puzzled, Sarah asked, "I don't understand. Why all the interest in those pills?"

"Why are there no lables on either bottle?" Albert asked.

"That's my medicine cabinet and I can't believe you're asking me questions about it!" After a pause, she explained, "Big bottles don't fit in that small cabinet, so I put a few pills in smaller bottles. But you aren't answering my question! Why all the interest in those pills?"

The two men looked at each other. Clarence spoke first; "You tell her, Albert."

Even with his mind still reeling from the letter, Albert managed to embellish the rescue story quite nicely. Clarence then added the events that happened in the house after they had escaped. When he described the noise that had awakened him, Albert punched his fist into the air. His trap had worked! It made him feel good that he had inflicted some pain on Sammy in his rush to stab the pillows.

Clarence paused, and then not knowing how else to tell the rest of the story, just told it the way it had happened. Since he never had been good at telling stories, he was pleasantly surprised to see both Albert and Sarah were laughing.

"Tell me again how many laxatives you gave him," she managed to get out between snorts.

"I smashed up five of each of those pills. So what was in the other bottle?" he asked.

Sarah had to sit down before she fell down. Wiping her eyes, she said. "Let me put it this way. If Sammy were a girl, and if this was her special time of the month, she wouldn't be having any cramps!"

Albert joined her on the ground. When it was obvious that Clarence didn't understand what she was talking about, they rolled together on the grass.

It took some time to sober up and come to grips with their situation. "We need help from town," Sarah stated. "The police have to be notified about Sammy. We can't do this by ourselves."

She turned to Albert. "I understand that you are the escaped prisoner." She had stated it bluntly, and she watched his face to see his reaction. "Begin by telling me why you were in jail in the first place."

Both men remained silent. Finally, a subdued Albert asked Clarence. "You wanna tell her?"

Clarence had been such a successful laxative storyteller that he sailed with confidence into their adventure of the four days in a pitch-dark garage. Sarah laughed and cheered when he described finding the doorknob that opened the access door to freedom. Albert wasn't finding it amusing.

"So, Albert, you went to jail, and I was in the beauty shop across the street the day you escaped. But Clarence, where were you?"

The two men looked at each other. Albert shrugged, turned to Clarence, and said, "She deserves to know."

Clarence nodded his head. "You tell it all, Albert."

Starting as far back as the incident in McGuire's Alley that had sent them to prison with Sammy in the first place, the sun had come up by the time Albert finished.

Sarah was quiet. "Albert, there has to be more to your story," she looked him in the eye. "I want to know what happened that made you leave the life you had with your mother. From the sound of the letter, your mother was a nice woman who had enough money to give you a good life. So how did you end up in a gang? It just doesn't make sense!"

He knew now was the time; he nodded and started the story back to where he made his first wrong choice. Somewhere an uncle who works for an organization with initials was still trying to find him for violating and ruining the life of the girl whose name Albert couldn't remember. One bad choice after another painted the not-so-pretty picture of Albert's life.

Sarah, appalled as she was by all that she had learned, knew that her survival depended on these two flawed men. Realizing they had spent far too much time in the sheltered area, she was feeling the urgent need to move on.

Looking at Albert's changed appearance, she had an idea. "Have you looked in the mirror since Sammy worked on you?" she asked him.

Clarence laughed. "He sure did. I'm surprised you didn't hear him yell while you were in that locked room!"

The mention of the locked room brought them all back to the present situation.

"Well, in case you've forgotten, I'll describe what I see. Your head is orange, your black brows look like caterpillars over your eyes, and your beard is growing in black."

"Wow! That's pretty bad!" Albert said, frowning.

"No, that's pretty good," said Sarah. "Since you look like my dead husband, I'm going to introduce you as his cousin. Let's see; you look like a Wendell. Yes, your name is Wendell Blakeman."

Satisfied with herself, she turned to Clarence. "Do the people in town know what you look like?"

Clarence thought. They would know him in that real estate office where they'd fixed him up after the bicycle crash, and the people in the restaurants they had stiffed by not paying their bills might recognize him, too. Oh yes, and there was the redheaded cop-snitch… but when he told her that all he was wanted for was home invasion and blowing up a microwave, she was derailed by laughter again.

"Pardon me, guys. I'm still dizzy from the fact that I'm alive. I'm sure the effect will wear off eventually," she said as she sobered up. "I don't know how to explain you, Clarence. We'll just have to play you by ear."

"You, too? I didn't know you could play with your ears! Albert can, you know!"

Sarah looked at Albert. "What's he talking about?"

"Don't pay any attention. Just forget he said that. So, have you come up with a plan?"

"I'm going to stand behind a tree out by the road and wait for some kind of official car to go by. No matter what direction it's going, I'm going to try to stop it. We need help, and we need it before Sammy finds us."

The two men agreed. They followed Sarah to the edge of the road where she found a good spot that would keep her out of sight but still be able see the traffic both coming and going. They concealed themselves further back in the brush.

Albert resigned himself to accept his fate. He knew it was time to end this part of their lives. Any outstanding debt to society would have to be paid in full and, in both their cases, it very likely meant more jail time. At the moment, jail time felt much safer than being found by Sammy.

A wave of homesickness reminded Albert how much he wanted to contact his mother.

CHAPTER 49

MITCH WAS STILL GROUSING when he spotted Tom and Marie standing beside their car, waiting to be picked up.

"How I ever let you talk me into a picnic this early in the morning, I'll never know. And what, pray tell, did you put in that picnic basket that's in the trunk? I didn't see you cooking anything that looked like picnic food!"

Molly squirmed. "Where is the romantic man I married not too long ago? I didn't think you'd turn into a sour old curmudgeon this soon!"

Mitch stopped the car long enough to let Marie and Tom crawl into the back seat, before he started again. "Tom, you aren't even married yet, and already you're letting Marie pull you around by the nose. I bet you think this picnic thing so early in the morning is as dumb as I think it is."

Tom was about to answer when he caught Marie's glare. "Well, as you said the other day, Mitch, sleep is highly overrated. And all I can say is there'd better be some pretty special food in the picnic basket! By the way, where is the basket?"

Molly didn't answer because she was intently peering out the window. Seeing the fire truck she was looking for, she called gaily, "Oh look Marie, there's your sister! Wonder what Clara and Joe are up to? They're waving for us to stop! What a coincidence!"

Against his better judgment, Mitch pulled off the road and stopped. Marie jumped out and ran to the truck, while gushing over the chance meeting of Joe and her sister, Clara.

Tom tapped Mitch on the shoulder. "I think we've been hoodwinked, buddy. Want to bet this is no accidental meeting?"

"Guess we're about to find out," Mitch grumbled as he climbed out of the car.

Joe stood back while Clara invited them all to ride on the fire truck while he took it out for a test run. While Molly and Marie excitedly accepted the invitation, Tom and Mitch remained silent.

Joe carefully pulled out into traffic and headed up the peninsula. Finally, Tom said, "Enough with the charade! What the hell are you ladies up to? And don't say a picnic. Even bears don't go on picnics this early in the morning! And Joe, you have to be in on this too. So why don't you be the one to enlighten the rest of us?"

"Uh, guys, uh, Clara made me see the logic in her, uh, theories, well, some of them anyway, and, uh, I agreed to go along with her, but not without backup."

"And we're the backup?" Mitch rolled his eyes.

"As it turns out, yeah," Joe answered, who right now was not feeling too friendly towards the girls who had gotten him into this wild goose chase. "And when Clara talked to Molly and Marie, she found that they both thought you guys had brushed off Clara's theories too soon."

Marie and Molly had the grace to blush.

"This is just great!" Mitch grumbled. "Is the vineyard the destination for this pretend picnic? Oh, by the way, the basket is still back in the trunk of my car." He turned to Molly. "There isn't any picnic food in that basket, is there?"

Molly hung her head.

Lucky was sitting by Joe, his head thrown back, and his ears were flopping in the wind. From the looks on everyone's face, Lucky was the only one enjoying the ride. His doggy sense told him something big was going to happen today; he could feel it in his bones.

Miles flew by smoothly. The old fire truck was back in good working order. The motley crew rode in silence.

Suddenly, something on the edge of the road caught Lucky's eye; he barked sharply. From the opposite side a woman ran out and stopped in the middle of the road, waving her arms. "Would you look at that nut? She's trying to get herself killed," Joe yelled as he slammed on the brakes.

"That's Sarah!" Clara shouted. "That's the owner of the vineyard where I think Sammy is hiding!"

The truck came to a skidding stop. "Oh, thank you, God!" sobbed the woman as the people and the dog jumped off the truck and surrounded her. Pandemonium, chaos, a barking dog, tears, questions, answers, hugs and a woman shouting, "I told you so" were the sound of safety to Sarah's ears; she suddenly felt weak with relief. It was over. She was saved.

The two men across the road debated when to announce their presence. The rescue group looked friendly enough, but both of them recognized the redheaded cop as the snitch in Sammy's gang. With a choice of jail or Sammy's knife, they picked jail.

One by one, the jabbering of the excited group stopped as they watched Albert and Clarence cross the road. Alarmed, Tom pulled out his gun. "Stop right there!" he ordered. "Not one more step!'

Sarah raced to stand in front of them. "These men are with me! Wendell is a cousin of my dead husband and Clarence is just a friend of the family. So please put down that gun!" she pleaded. "We know where Sammy the Grunt is, so save your bullets for him!"

Clara, whose crazy theories had just been vindicated, was jumping up and down shouting, "I told you so! I told yo…"

Mitch pushed her aside. "Later, Clara!" he commanded.

"Hey, don't push!" she complained as she stepped back. "I'll take this up with you later!" She turned to the rest of the gang and mouthed the words, "I told you so!"

Mitch took a step towards Sarah. "Are you saying you know where Sammy is right now?"

"You mean at this very moment?" Sarah asked. "I imagine he's around here somewhere trying to find me. Wendell helped me escape out the window, but I would imagine he's still looking for me, so he's not far away."

The man called Wendell spoke up. "Eventually he'll give up lookin' for us and go back to the vineyard. We can wait for him there, but you're gonna have to ditch the truck someplace." He grinned, and added. "It's hard to sneak up on someone when you're drivin' a fire truck!"

It was a crowded truck that headed for the vineyard. Sarah had quit shaking but her empty stomach wouldn't let her forget it needed food. Timidly she asked, "Would you possibly have any food with you? Since Sammy intended to kill me, he hasn't been feeding me. I'm really hungry."

Shocked, the women looked at each other. What had started out as a lark, playing a trick on their men to get them to the vineyard, had suddenly turned serious. Maybe they hadn't given this project enough thought; maybe they hadn't taken into consideration the kind of evil they were about to meet. What if their little plan was going to get someone killed?

Molly, thinking of Laurie, Kim, and the twins back home in Anita's care, tapped Mitch on the shoulder. "Maybe we should stop and think this through before we go any further."

"It's a bit late for second thoughts," Mitch answered, "the vineyard is just around the next turn."

Joe had already found a spot to hide the truck. No one spoke, and no one made a move to get off. Mitch cleared his throat, "Uh, Tom, do you have any idea what we're doing?"

"Not a clue," admitted Tom. "There's safety in numbers, and since I have the only gun, stay close to me. And Clara, take Lucky off his chain. If this dog has been standing guard the past few days looking for Sammy, let's give him a chance."

Walking the last quarter mile, Tom engaged the cousin, the man with the orange hair and the black eyebrows, in conversation. He figured if he could get the guy named Wendell to talk, he would figure out why he looked familiar.

"Wendell," said Tom, "I'm puzzled. I don't understand how the three of you got away from Sammy, and why he never caught up with you."

"Clarence and I knew Sammy intended to kill Sarah last night because he told us," Albert said. "So Clarence smashed up some pills we found in Sarah's bathroom and put them in Sammy's dinner. We were hopin' they were sleepin' pills, but they weren't."

"What were they if they weren't sleeping pills?"

"Laxatives! And the reason Sammy didn't catch us was because he couldn't leave the bathroom!"

Tom had to stop walking because he was laughing. "Hey, gang, wait up! You have to hear this!"

Tom told the story with color and embellishments and the mood of the group lightened a bit. Then, silently and in single file, they stayed in cover as much as possible as they approached the house. Sarah, safely in the middle of the group, looked up at the window to her room. The hours she had spent looking out that window with no hope of rescue were fresh in her memory. She wondered if she could ever erase the essence of Sammy from her house. One thing she knew, never again would she sleep in her old bedroom. As her legs failed her, Molly, sensing Sarah's emotion, steadied her with a hug. Sarah gave her a thankful smile.

Almost abreast of the shed, she stopped. The man called Wendell, who was still talking to Tom, bumped into her.

"Alb….Wendell," she said quietly, "could I have a word with you?"

"Now?" he asked, surprised."

"Yes, now." Sarah had an edge to her voice.

"I guess so," he replied, "but couldn't it wait until we find Sammy?"

"Now!" she said as she pulled him off to the side. "Albert, there's one detail we haven't talked about."

Albert looked confused. "I thought me and Clarence confessed to everything. What did we miss?"

"I don't know," Sarah hissed. "You tell me."

"Hey, come on, now!" Albert looked hurt. "Give me a clue!"

Sarah looked him in the eye. "I was remembering being in the bedroom and looking out that window," she said, pointing up. "And I remembered one night when I watched the man I knew as Frank take food and clothes to someone in that shed."

Albert hung his head. "That was me in the shed," he said quietly.

"That's what I figured." Sarah thought for a moment and then asked, "Albert, after you escaped from jail, how did you get from town to my shed?"

"You brought me," he answered so quietly she had trouble hearing the words.

"Did I hear you right?" she asked, her voice raised. This brought stares from the group that was waiting for the two to finish their conversation.

"Yes, you brought me. I had to hide fast, and there was your truck across the street, all loaded with supplies. I hid under the netting."

Sarah's mouth dropped open in shock. Speechless, she closed her eyes and swayed. Albert put his hand on her shoulder to steady her.

Finally finding her voice, she said, "I'm having trouble believing all this was just a coincidence. Did you know where the truck would take you?"

"I had no idea," he admitted. "You can't imagine how surprised I was when I heard Sammy and Clarence's voices."

She shook her head. "How did all this happen? I get rescued by people I've never seen before…except for that one who keeps shouting, 'I told you so!' I saw her that day in the beauty shop. Wonder how she figured out that Sammy was living at my vineyard?"

"I think the dog figured it out," Albert said, scratching his orange head.

"Oh, come on, Albert, who told you that story?" she let out a short laugh. "This is not the time for kidding around. Sammy is out there somewhere and I hope no one thinks he's going to be glad to see us!"

"No, honest!" Albert crossed his heart. "I didn't make that up! I heard them talking."

"Sure you did," Sarah said, unconvinced.

The dog in question was running up and down the rows of vines, his nose to the ground. "Do you think Lucky is on to something?" Joe asked Clara.

"If Sammy's here, he's gonna find him!" Clara assured him. "I brought my camera just in case."

Joe blinked. "You're serious? You brought your camera so that you can take pictures of Sammy if Lucky catches him?"

"I need more business!" Clara explained. "Lucky hasn't done anything outrageous since he attacked Santa last Christmas!"

Joe just shook his head.

Molly marveled as they approached the vineyard, "So this is how they grow grapes. Can't say I've ever been in a vineyard before."

Sarah cast a critical eye at the dog that was racing around her tidy rows of vines. The grass had been mowed and the weeds pulled. How nice it was that, while she was locked in her room, the men had tended her vineyard. Then it dawned on her. Of course! Sammy only had to do away with her and the vineyard would be his. Why wouldn't he tend it?

Anger such as she had never felt before shook her.

A low growl from Lucky got their attention. Down one row toward the end, they saw the figure of a man crouched low, moaning softly, his trousers puddled around his feet. He was so engrossed that he didn't even hear them all approaching.

"Yipes! I think we're being mooned!" Tom snorted.

"Clara, I hope you have your camera ready!" hissed Joe, "but I don't think these pictures will be suitable for a family newspaper!"

Suddenly, Lucky sprinted between the rows of vines, heading for the crouched man. Sammy, his face contorted, was in the middle of a gut-spasm when he heard the sound of pounding feet. Looking over his shoulder, he saw a creature straight out of a bad nightmare running towards him. Hindered by the trousers bunched around his shoes, he tried to run while frantically pulling them up over his bare behind.

"No, no, no!" Sammy cried, looking over his shoulder, "Git away, dog! What th…?" he yelled as Lucky leaped.

The group arrived at the scene to see Lucky stretched out over the protesting man.

LUCKY GRINNED FOR Clara when she took the picture. The readers of tomorrow's newspaper where going to love this story. The phones at Allen Real Estate were going to ring again.

Sammy the Grunt, the king of all gang leaders, the man whose very name struck fear into the hearts of men, the man whose skill with the knife was legendary, had been brought down by laxatives and a mongrel dog.

And Clara had pictures to prove it.

EPILOGUE

THE WEATHER WAS PERFECT, the sky was blue, and the clouds were white. The little church was picture-postcard-perfect for what was happening inside.

Sounds of rolling organ music and the heady perfume of flowers drifted back to the vestibule where the bride and her attendants were doing a last-minute check before walking down the aisle. Both sides of the church were filled.

The groom and his best man entered the sanctuary from a side door. As they turned to watch for the bride and her entourage, a murmur rose up from the congregation. The groom was glowing. A beam of sunlight had made its way through the stained glass window and lit up his red hair.

Today, Tom Allen was marrying Marie Clark. His best man, Joe Skinner, was as anxious as Tom for the procession to begin, because Clara, who was wearing his ring, would be walking down the aisle, too. She was Marie's sister and her maid of honor.

Joe's eye scanned the congregation searching for his two boys. He had full custody of them now that Brenda's new true love wanted nothing to do with them. They had promised to be on their best behavior if he allowed them to come to the wedding; sometimes their idea of what was best was questionable. Their squirming stopped when they felt the steely eyes of their dad.

Albert, seated at the organ playing softly, was ready to switch to 'Here Comes the Bride' as soon as the bride appeared. He smiled as he watched Clarence, all spiffed out in a tux and loving every minute of his ushering job, hurrying some late arrivals to their seats. Then his eyes searched the crowd until he found his mother sitting beside Sarah, who, feeling his eyes on her, looked up and smiled at him. The distance between them did not diminish the effect of the ignited spark. The charge was enough to make Albert forget what song he was playing.

The back door opened and the first of the bridal party started down the aisle. Clara and Molly drew appreciative murmurs in their emerald green dresses. The color of the dress matched the green of Molly's eyes, eyes that no longer were marred by dark circles. Dr. Parker had worked his magic again. Of course, the bride was beautiful. The bridal party that gathered in front of the minister was truly splendid, but the ring bearer stole the show.

Lucky, all decked out in a stiff white collar and bow tie, marched up the aisle. He stood still until Joe untied the pouch that was hanging around his neck and removed the ring. Knowing his job was finished, Lucky turned and walked to the back. The applause started hesitantly, but quickly caught on. Maybe it wasn't a proper thing to do in church, but for Lucky, they applauded with enthusiasm.

Albert and Clarence had paid their debt to society. Home invasion, a blown-up microwave, an injured Church Lady, and Albert's escape from jail were now marked "Paid in Full". The Church Lady had refused to press charges if Albert agreed to become the church organist, and the homeowner, who happened to be a member of the same church, forgave Clarence for ruining his microwave. Uncle Bill, the man who worked for the organization with initials, had been killed in a drug raid and Albert had not been successful in his attempt to find the girl whose life he had ruined. This, he would regret to the end of his days.

After a short stay in jail, both men had been welcomed back to the vineyard to help Sarah with the grape harvest.

That fall, when the grapes were purple and full of juice, Albert thought about his dad.

CPSIA information can be obtained at www.ICGtesting.com
233287LV00001B/4/P

9 781614 342854